Dreams Never End

Dreams Never End

new noir short stories

edited by
Nicholas Royle

**Tindal
Street
Press**

First published in 2004 by
Tindal Street Press Ltd,
217 The Custard Factory, Gibb Street, Birmingham B9 4AA.
www.tindalstreet.co.uk

A CIP catalogue reference for this book is available from
the British Library.

ISBN 0 9547913 0 4

Typesetting by Country Setting, Kingsdown, Kent.
Printed and bound in Great Britain by Clays Ltd, St Ives PLC.

Contents

Introduction

Images of chaos recur throughout these stories. The lights of Birmingham are 'smeared . . . into white and gold streaks by the weak indecisive rain'. More rain, in another story, produces 'weeping smears of colour, rumours of shape struggling to find form beyond the sluicing wipers'. We witness various characters in the act of fleeing from chaos, often of their own making. Sometimes it's the chaos of unreason: an unexplained epidemic of female suicides, a woman with pink pants and a penis, a man starting a fire on impulse in his neighbour's house. At other times, the potential for chaos, the possibility of havoc, rests in a gun in a bedside drawer, fondled for comfort, representing a dream of release.

The characters we meet – a young prostitute, an asylum seeker, a bunch of gangsters and a pair of eccentric detectives, among others – are all damaged dreamers. Circumstance has, to varying extents, made them what they are. Some retain a trace of the innate goodness with which they set out; a few have had it beaten out of them by the time we meet them. Others lose the capacity for moral behaviour, in exchange for a little insight and not much more, in the course of their story. We should not sit in judgement, however, for there but by the grace of God . . .

God? Moral standards are a luxury in 'the stone-cold heart of a visceral metropolis' where people make their own mistakes and others suffer for them. The lighting may produce the stark chiaroscuro of noir cinema, but the moral landscape is painted in shades of grey. No one is as pure as the driven snow, which in 'a city of dark, illuminated rain' turns to slush, and even the most callous assassin may yet be saved. Indeed, many of these characters have dreams of saving themselves, or at least dreams of escape. Practical attempts to break free of their nightmarish circumstances inevitably meet resistance, but dreams never end. The human spirit, while it may dwindle, is never quite extinguished.

This showcase anthology presents three very different writers with three quite distinct takes on contemporary noir. Andrew Newsham is as much at home in the gangster-infested no-go areas of New York's outer boroughs or the suburbs of any other major US city as he is in the mean streets of Birmingham (not Alabama), although where 'The Party Trick' and 'Teaching a New Dog Old Tricks' are set is anybody's guess. Everywhere, and nowhere. Their universality is their strength. That and Newsham's ability to make you laugh, even when the subject matter is as dark as it gets.

Mick Scully initiates profound moral investigations into the lives of his characters, whose dramas evolve from the villains' pubs, canal towpaths and depreived housing estates of the West Midlands. Scully's Birmingham is a harsh environment in which all your choices are difficult ones and those who have elected to follow a life of crime drink together in the Little Moscow.

H P Tinker has been described as a writer of 'comic existentialist crime' and the 'Thomas Pynchon of Chorlton-cum-Hardy'. His is a world in which the police have no better an understanding of what is happening than the victims of a crime, and in which a detective's partner is liable to be killed unexpectedly in a tragic accident with a minibus carrying a jazz quartet. It's an absurd world drenched in noir, in which melancholy is a perfume and a quick hop on a train amounts to your being 'gripped by an addiction to the melancholy of solitary travel through the cold dark cities of the world'.

It's hard to believe, when you come across work as powerful, original and richly varied as this, that the short story is fiction's most endangered species. As long as there are publishers bold enough to stick with shorts through the lean times, writers as committed and adventurous as the present company, and – perhaps most importantly – readers who still seek the rare thrill of a well-told tale, the short story will continue to work its peculiar magic.

Nicholas Royle
September 2004

Andrew Newsham

ANDREW NEWSHAM was born in Burnley, but now lives in Birmingham, where he is writing his first novel, *Disorganised Crime*. After a brief spell as a journalist he decided to follow the example of his literary heroes: to explore the world and to write. He won the *Esquire* prize for short fiction in 2001 and was the first writer from Europe to be invited to America by the Jack Kerouac Writers in Residence project in 2003.

The Nazi Gold
Andrew Newsham

We'd been called out to the Boss's cabin. Something big was going down. There were rumours we were going to war with Don Francisco who was in charge of one of the most powerful families. Everyone was tense.

Frank, Mickey Boosh and Monster were playing cards at the table. I was sat at the counter reading the sports pages and trying to take my mind off things. I knew something bad was going to happen and that we'd have to do it, like the time when we chopped off Gino's hands down by the stream because he'd been skimming off the bakery money. It still haunted me, the screams, the way he pleaded as we tightened the tourniquets.

Pablo was pacing up and down on the creaky porch and playing with his gun. He'd walk from one end to the other, then swivel round, put the gun to his head and pull the trigger. It would click on an empty chamber and then he'd start walking again. There was a faraway look in his eyes, and the creaky floorboards made it sound like we were all adrift on a Spanish galleon.

Frank was losing at cards and I could see Pablo was getting to him.

'For crying out loud,' he shouted, 'will you stop fucking about for two fucking minutes?'

Pablo stopped moving and stared through the open door at the clock on the wall for exactly two minutes. Then he started up again.

Mickey Boosh and Monster laughed.

'You fucking child,' said Frank, staring at his cards.

Pablo kept right on with his routine and then, after three or four more turns, he came into the room and stopped behind Frank and let off the gun right at the back of his head. Frank jumped up and pulled out his own gun from its holster.

'Take it easy, old man,' said Pablo, grinning like a lunatic.

'Give me one good reason why I shouldn't put a cap in your ass?'

They glared at each other for a few seconds and I suppose it could have gotten ugly but then Carlos came in from the main house.

'What's going on?' he asked.

'Puerto Rican shit, you know what it's like,' said Monster in his snide way.

Carlos grimaced. He was from our neighbourhood and was always touchy about what anyone said about us; we were just beginning to get ahead in the organization and it wasn't easy. The Italians still ruled as a matter of course and the Irish had their cop connections, but what did we have? Our people still bought live fucking chickens for Chrissake. It pissed him off. Nine times out of ten it was our guys who got their fingers burnt in the fires; it was our guys who got shot first. We were the cannon fodder henchmen, the first guys to die. That's one thing the movies did get right.

'OK, listen up,' he said and called us all in to the table where he spread out a map.

Boosh and Monster stood up and wandered off a little way. They were only the Boss's bodyguards and this was a real piece of work.

'OK, time for you to make up for all those fuck-ups you've been bringing down on us.' Carlos liked using us, but I could tell sometimes that we embarrassed him. Like this one time when we killed the wrong Fat Tony. I mean, how were we supposed to know? Fat white guys all looked the same to us.

I climbed off my stool and looked at the map. It was a detailed rendering of the docks.

'A boat has arrived from Europe,' said Carlos. 'They've dropped off a crate that belongs to Don Francisco. We want it.'

Monster groaned as soon as he heard the Don's name. He was no coward but he'd lost two brothers the last time the families had serious hostilities.

'Shut the fuck up,' said Carlos.

'But won't that start a war?' asked Frank.

'It would do, if we sent someone who regularly worked for the Boss. But we're not. We're sending you guys. And you've got to wear masks.'

'What kind of masks?' asked Pablo.

'The transparent kind that help people see your face, you dumb fuck,' said Carlos.

Pablo said, 'I'm not putting my head in no woman's tights.'

'Look, I don't care what you do, just make sure that nobody can see your face,' said Carlos.

He outlined the plan for us. It sounded easy. We had a mole in Don Francisco's gang. He'd leave us the keys to the truck with the crate we wanted on the back. All we had to do was kill a couple of guards and drive the truck away. There was even a way into the compound through a hole in a fence.

'What's in the crate?' asked Frank.

'Nazi gold,' said Carlos.

'Where do we take it?'

'The Stone Yard in Queens.'

'That doesn't sound too safe.'

'It's safe enough. We can't take it to our places in case the Don finds it and we get all the families stomping on our heads.'

'So where do we get the masks?' asked Pablo.

'Pull them out of your mother's ass for all I care. Now get the fuck out of here. Don Francisco is flying back from Florida tonight so you've got to get that gold before he lands.'

We drove back to the city in Frank's Mustang. He made us listen to Johnny Cash all the way but it didn't matter much because we were too busy worrying about our mission. It didn't look good. We were only being used because we were expendable and if it all went wrong then the Boss would deny that he had anything to do with us. We might be killed anyway because we were the only ones who could link the heist back to the Boss.

Frank found a 7–Eleven on the way to the docks and pulled up outside. I went in and asked if there were any Halloween masks but it was the wrong season and they didn't have shit so I bought a few pairs of tights.

Back in the car Pablo said he wouldn't wear them.

'Why not?' asked Frank.

'I don't like 'em.'

'You're really starting to piss me off,' said Frank.

'I can't do it. They make me think of pussy. I don't want to be killing nobody when I'm thinking of pussy. I don't want to get fucked up in the head, end up back in the padded room.'

'You're already fucked up enough,' said Frank.

'I've got to take steps to protect my mental health.'

'I don't believe this . . . What were you doing the other day when I came up to your place? You were running around the fucking chicken coop on the top of that tenement block like some goddamn werewolf. You think that's normal? At least this is work.'

Pablo looked out of the car window and frowned. We'd have to get something else for him. There was no way we could do the job without him.

'There's this costume shop in the East Village,' I said.

'No, I got a better idea,' said Frank and he drove us down the street to a sports bar.

'What are you doing?' I said.

'I know this place, it's got all kinds of hockey masks and shit stuck to the walls.'

I got out the car with Frank, but Pablo stayed in the front seat and maintained a frosty air of indifference.

'Fucking prima donna,' said Frank.

'We're running out of time,' I said.

Frank said, 'So let's go in there and take a mask and come back out and nail it to that fucker's head. And fast.'

It was your standard sports bar: televisions everywhere, waitresses in skin-tight Lycra. Jocks drinking jugs of beer and giving each other high fives for making asinine quips. I didn't like sport and I didn't like these places. For all I was concerned this bit of America could go straight to hell. I never fit into this slice of the dream. They said there was no colour bar but there was really. At school the men who liked these places used sport as an excuse to punch me.

We walked in and a waitress asked us where we wanted to sit.

'Near some hockey masks,' said Frank.

The waitress walked us to some tables where there was a big screen showing a hockey game.

'No,' said Frank. 'We're not interested in the game of hockey, only the protective equipment.'

She didn't know what to do but I saw a mask in a glass case and I nudged Frank and we sat down at the nearest table and told the waitress to bring some beer and chicken wings.

We stared at the mask a while. It was awesome: a big brown leather affair, full face and patched together with evil-looking stitches. It turned out it was the mask of some famous goalkeeper called the Butcher. He was notoriously violent and had won lots of trophies. It was perfect for Pablo. I could just imagine him wearing it while he played with his chainsaw.

Before I knew what was happening Frank had stormed over to the mask and smashed the glass with the butt of his gun. There was uproar and alarms sounded and out of nowhere this bunch of guys ran over and pinned Frank up against the wall with some serious handguns. It turned out to be the SWAT team's office party. Of all the dumb fucking luck.

I was a bit behind the action and I managed to duck round some pinball machines and sneak out of a fire door into the parking lot. There was no point both of us getting arrested or worse. Especially as we still had the job to do.

I sprinted round to the car and found Pablo in the driver's seat revving the engine.

'Where's Frank?' he asked.

I jumped in the back and told him to go. 'The place was crawling with cops . . .'

He thought about it for a few seconds. I could see he wanted to go in and get Frank, guns blazing.

'Don't worry, he'll get bail, it's nothing,' I said.

He popped the clutch and we shot off down the road, passing a police car coming the other way with all its lights flashing like a Vegas casino.

We drove around a bit and I told him what had happened and how we'd have to do the job alone and how we were running out of time and he was going to have to wear the tights.

He was really pissed off. I don't know what burned him more, the fact that he'd have to wear the tights or that he'd have to do the job with me on his own. I was just a kid really but I promised him I was ready to 'step up to the plate' and that he could count on me.

'OK,' said Pablo, 'but fuck up or even look like fucking up and I'll gut you like a fish.'

'Don't worry,' I said. I was trying to sound cool but my stomach was doing somersaults.

We arrived at the docks at around two. I found the hole in the fence and crept in. It was just like Carlos said it would be, only the truck didn't have two guards, it had four and they were stood around an oil-drum fire, bitching about how they would rather be somewhere else. They also had semi-automatics. Something else we hadn't figured on.

I went back to the car and gave Pablo the bad news.

He didn't say anything, he just went and got Frank's automatic shotgun from the trunk.

'This should even things up,' he said.

He gave me his Mauser and we put the tights on the top of our heads, ready to pull down when required.

'If I get a boner,' he said, 'I'll kick your ass.'

I started to lead him through to the hole in the fence. It was then that he made me promise that if he ended up in the nut-house I'd do all that I could to get him out.

'Sure,' I said.

He grabbed my arm. 'Promise.'

'I promise, man. You're not going to end up in a mental institution just cus you wear some tights on your head . . .'

He looked at me and there was real fear in his eyes. I suddenly felt sorry for him. He was a cold-blooded killer but it must have been hell for him sometimes, fighting the bubbling insanity inside him. It was a touching moment and then it was over and he pulled down the tights over his face and we crept into the compound and he did what he always did best.

He saw the four guys stood around the bin and just marched right up and shot them down in a spray of bullets. They never stood a chance. One of them got as far as to turn on us but I shot him in the chest and he died.

It was my first kill, but I like to see it now as self-defence. He'd have shot me if I hadn't shot him.

When everyone was dead Pablo told me to take the truck and go. There was a weird tone to his voice. He was excited.

'GO NOW,' he rasped, panting heavily and sniffing at the tights on his face like a pervert.

I was relieved to get out of his way.

When they found the headless bodies, everyone said it was a 'nice touch' because the rumour mill naturally blamed it on the Haitians.

I'd never driven a truck before but the key was waiting for me, just like Carlos said it would be, and I managed to fight the controls and get the thing rolling. I got to the Stone Yard without incident, and I called Carlos. I made it sound like it all went without a hitch. He was pleased and said the boss would be right over and I should just 'hang tight'.

I couldn't stop myself having a look at the gold, though. My head was full of pictures of some Egyptian king's tomb or something but when I opened up the truck I was seriously disappointed. There was nothing inside but a couple of clothes racks full of Nazi uniforms and a load of funny-looking table lamps. I picked one up and studied it. It was lightweight and certainly wasn't gold. I realized it was made of human skin and bone.

I damn near fainted. I'm sad to admit that it wasn't from the shock of the Holocaust craftwork, but more from the fear of having to explain to the Boss that there was no gold.

What if we'd taken the wrong truck? What if the Boss thought we'd stolen the gold? If he so much as thought we'd fucked up or tried to screw him we'd all be dead in a matter of hours.

I didn't know what to do. There was no point running because that would be seen as confirmation of my guilt. By the time the Boss arrived I'd climbed up on top of the truck thinking it was sort of a safe place. At least I would be out of reach when they saw there was no gold. The boss wasn't known for his sense of humour.

I told them what happened and they listened to me quite calmly, but I knew they were pissed. They wanted me to climb off the truck to talk to them. I told them I wouldn't until I was sure they believed me. It went on like that for a while until Monster climbed up and threw me down. I twisted my ankle and took a few slaps until Pablo arrived and we talked it all out. He backed up everything I said and we somehow got them to believe we hadn't made a switch.

'They're too dumb to try anything like that,' said Monster.

'Or too loyal,' said Carlos.

Someone called the police to check on Frank and it was this, the dumb fucking stupidity of him being pinched, that saved us. His time of arrest fitted our story so precisely that it just couldn't have happened any other way.

The boss made us bury the Nazi stuff in the woods but when Frank got out of jail we all needed some money because we were out in the cold again. So he made me take him to where we'd buried it and we dug it all up and we sold it to some guy who ended up passing it on to some prop collector for the movies. The shit turned up in some pretty major films and looking out for it became one of Frank's obsessions. I don't think he ever watched a film properly after that. Every other scene he'd stop the tape and study the background furniture. He was always on the lookout for the stuff, the hideous ghost of history forever obscuring the frame.

Teaching a New Dog Old Tricks

Andrew Newsham

I was sat on my usual stool at the bar when a kid walked in with this whole rockabilly thing going on. His hair was fixed in a sharp quiff and he wore a tight blue velvet coat. He had the look perfect, right down to the winkle-pickers on his feet. The fifties were my original era and now it was 'the look' once more. Some band had made it popular again. They stole the style and made out they were doing something new. It was certainly a new way to get at young people's money. It almost made me wish I'd kept all my old clothes.

He looked the place over cautiously before deciding to approach the bar. I smiled at him but he ignored me. I couldn't understand young people. They seemed smart but confused at the same time. They had everything and still contrived to be miserable.

'Beer, please,' he said, nodding towards one of the pumps.

Floyd looked at him in disbelief for a few moments. 'You got ID?'

The kid fumbled nervously around in his coat pockets before pulling out a laminated piece of card.

Floyd eyed the ID suspiciously before grabbing a glass and pouring a beer.

'And a whiskey,' said the kid.

He pulled a black wallet out of his coat pocket and paid with a twenty.

On a quiet night the cash register didn't care who fed it. If the police came in Floyd would just act like an idiot and say the ID had fooled him.

The kid took a sip of his beer.

'Hot date tonight?' I asked. He smiled but made no reply. 'Or is it your birthday?'

'You were right the first time,' he said. He took all his change from the bar and put his wallet back in his coat pocket.

'Good on you,' I said. 'Got to get it while you can. But let me tell you something, don't get hung up on one woman. Make sure you spread your love around while you're still young. Not a man alive who didn't wish he'd had more women.'

'No problem there,' said the kid.

The sweet smell of some fancy cologne pricked my nostrils. Maybe his head was full of nonsense about 'love' and her being 'the one' and all that naïve stuff. I decided to put him straight.

'You're young, you don't realize it, but a lot of chances will come your way. You're so keyed up that you're liable to fixate and I guarantee she will be the wrong one.'

The kid raised his eyebrows and drew out a crumpled pack of cigarettes.

I looked at my glass. It was ringed heavily with froth; I'd been drinking slow because I'd run out of money. Floyd wasn't letting me have any more credit until I'd got my tab down to under a hundred again. He said I was going to put him out of business. Truth was, on some days I was the only business. I drained the last sip of beer and set the empty glass slowly back on the bar.

'Look,' I said, 'I've been married three times and I've been in prison twice and I might not look up to much now but I've got a head full of diamonds and if you feel like buying me a beer I won't mind sharing 'em with you.'

The kid smiled. 'Go on then,' he said.

Floyd set about pouring me another.

I took a swig of the fresh draught and smacked my lips.

'Nothing like a nice cold one after a hard day's drinking,' said Floyd, walking off down to the TV at the end of the bar where he was watching the hockey.

'Now I can tell by the way you've come in here,' I said to the kid, 'that you're eager and that's no bad thing but it ain't necessarily good either. Tell me, do you think she's "the one"?'

He blushed and shook his head. 'No,' he said.

'Well, good for you,' I said. 'I'm glad you're keeping something in reserve. Just be careful that you don't get caught out. The first spell I did in prison was over a woman. I was married but I lost it big time for this blonde teacher. It was crazy, I couldn't think straight. The wife found out and waited until I was asleep one night and then tried to castrate me with a pair of scissors. In self-defence I threw her against the wall and she hit her head and died. I lost one ball, four pints of blood and five years of my life.'

'Unlucky,' said the kid coolly.

'Luck had nothing to do with it. I let myself down. A man is always primarily at war with himself. Right now there are chemicals flowing through your bloodstream that could Shanghai you into all kinds of unwholesome situations.'

The kid looked a bit bemused. Floyd walked back up the bar and plucked a stick of spicy sausage from a jar next to the cash register.

'Floyd knows what I'm talking about,' I said.

'What's that?' he said, tearing off a corner of the wrapper with his teeth.

'Testosterone,' I said.

He rolled his eyes and walked off, chewing the sausage like a hungry dog. 'Oh yeah, testosterone,' he barked. 'GOD DAMN THAT TESTOSTERONE.' He was clearly getting into the hockey.

'I bet you don't know it, but right now you're flooded with testosterone and it's good for nothing but making you fuck or fight or go bald.' I took off my hat and showed him the big bare dome of my head.

He laughed. 'Nice.'

'It could happen to you,' I said.

I watched him as he got stuck into his beer, drinking it down in big hasty gulps. Drinking the whiskey made him look older than he was. The beer showed he was still just a pup.

'Of course,' I continued after a while, 'it's a lot worse if you're stuck on just one woman. When you start to feel that particular bite then you're at your weakest. If a woman can sense that, you're little better than a slave.'

He made no comment and we sat in silence. Eventually he finished his pint and shot and ordered a couple more, paying again with another note fresh from his wallet. He left me hanging with about a third of my beer left. Where did a young punk like that get his money?

I could really have gone for a whiskey.

Floyd looked at me. I shook my head and he walked away without filling my glass.

The kid pulled out his cigarettes, lit one and then looked at his watch. Maybe the girl was going to stand him up. I can't say I blamed her; he wasn't much of a conversationalist.

'If she doesn't turn up, just count it as a lucky escape,' I said.

He sighed. 'So you think women are essentially duplicitous creatures out to lead us into folly for their own wicked gain?'

'Well, yes. Very finely put,' I said. Duplicitous. The boy had certainly had an education. Daddy was probably a lawyer or something. I wondered what it cost to have words like that dropped into your mouth at birth.

'So why don't you tell me something I don't know?' he asked. He was turning into Dr Jekyll and Mr Wise Ass with every sip of alcohol.

'I'm just getting to that,' I said. 'As I was saying, the time will come when you'll get hooked by a woman and then you'll thank me for what I'm going to tell you.' I took a drink and cast my mind back to when I was twenty years old and I was in love with a girl called Maria Bertoli. I'd had a quiff a lot larger than this kid at the bar, but otherwise we were quite similar.

'My first love was truly breathtaking. At one time I'd have done anything for her, even cut off my own arms.'

'Why would she ask you to do that?' he said sarcastically.

'It's just an expression,' I said, ignoring his petulance. 'She had the biggest tits I've ever seen in my life. I needed two hands to tackle one. It was like trying to strangle a weather balloon. Two weather balloons.'

'The romance.'

'Nipples like round brown bullets. They were incredible . . .'

'I believe you.'

'But they weren't why I fell for her. They weren't even a factor, actually. It was her nose. She had the cutest nose. Small and pointed and ever so slightly pinched. Up till the day I met her I don't think I'd ever looked at a woman's nose. After her, every other nose seemed ugly or ridiculous. I discovered her body and those breasts later, but it was the nose I really loved.'

The kid waved Floyd over and ordered another whiskey for himself and left me hanging again. When he'd been served I continued.

'At least, I thought there was nothing on earth like that nose but I was soon proved wrong. I was on my way to see her one day and I had to get two trams and I always took her a present of some flowers. I liked to imagine that nose in action. It gave me a boner, made the journey go quicker.'

Behind us the door opened and the kid turned round eagerly but it was just an old woman with a bucket full of roses. She took one look at the empty bar and turned to leave.

'No wait,' the kid called after her. He jumped off his stool and bought a rose. He paid with another note and let her keep the change. The kid had money to burn.

When he sat back down he looked pretty pleased with himself.

'As a matter of fact, on that day I took her some roses too,' I said before continuing with my story. 'I was on my second tram when this fat guy sat down next to me. He was so huge he pressed right up to me, so I could almost feel the fabric of his pants straining.'

I paused and caught the kid playing with his mobile phone under the bar. I guess I was a relic, of little interest to a kid like him. I could remember when you had to send telegrams, delivered by hand. Incredible when you think about it.

'Go on,' he said without looking up.

'Well . . . I'd never met him before but the instant I set eyes on him I thought he looked familiar, not merely familiar but astoundingly striking.'

'What year was it?' he asked casually as he slipped his phone into the inside pocket of his jacket.

As soon as he asked the question I took the opportunity to lean across to him and grab his arm.

'It was 1955,' I said, looking deep into his eyes. He nodded his head and pulled backwards and I let him go. He brushed the arm of his jacket where I'd touched it as if I'd dirtied him somehow.

I sat back silently and didn't utter another word.

'So what happened next?' he asked after a while.

'Where was I?'

'On the bus.'

'Tram, it was all trams in those days,' I said.

'Yeah, tram, donkey, whatever.'

I cleared my throat. 'We set off and I began to dream about Maria's nose, how I would soon feel it poking into my moustache as I kissed her and then it came to me how I'd recognized the fat man. If I'd been a cartoon a flashing lightbulb would have suddenly appeared over my head.' I turned and caught the kid's eye. 'He had exactly the same nose as Maria,' I said.

'What do you mean?'

'The nose, the beautiful nose. At the time it was quite a shock.'

He shrugged and took a gulp of beer like he was drinking orange cordial.

'I don't get it,' he said.

'It's obvious,' I said. 'Women always seem better than they really are. You think they've got something unique but whatever it is, be prepared for that day when you're sat on a tram and the fat guy next to you has exactly the same nose.'

The kid said nothing. I guess he didn't think it was much of a story.

Floyd wiped the bar with his cloth. He stood listening to the silence building up between us before he spoke.

'Why don't you tell him about your second wife?' he said.

'What about my second wife?' I said.

'You know, why you left her.'

'She started to look like a fish, a big puff-eyed fish,' I said. I picked up the last of my pitiful beer and finished it off. 'I agreed for richer or poorer only, not poorer and looking like a big puff-eyed fish.'

Floyd looked at the kid and winked. 'Yeah, but what about in sickness or in health?'

'What about it?'

'Well, maybe her facial appearance was the result of some illness.'

'Look, I'm not going to discuss whether or not her appearance, her sudden monstrous descent into fishiness, was or was not the result of an illness, I just know I never agreed to it . . .'

As I spoke the kid suddenly jumped off his stool and started patting down his pockets.

'What the fuck?' he said as he went over his pockets again. Floyd watched him closely. I played it cool.

'What's wrong?' Floyd asked.

'My wallet. I've lost my wallet,' he said angrily, shooting me a mean glance.

'Don't look at me,' I said.

'You old fuck,' he said, patting down his pockets again.

'It must have been that rose woman. Gypsies have nimble fingers.'

'Shit,' he said.

I got off my stool. 'Look, if you think I've got it why don't you check my pockets?'

He was just about to take me up on my offer when his date arrived. She was twice his age, a real vamp. She was dressed in the fifties look as well, with a circle skirt and a pointy-bra sweater. It suited her.

'Hey honey, what's the matter?' she asked.

'This guy just stole my wallet,' he said.

'I did no such thing.'

'Why don't you empty your pockets on the bar?' suggested Floyd. I slowly turned out all my pockets. Naturally his wallet wasn't there, just a bunch of coupons, some keys, a half pack of mints, an old bus ticket. If fluff were money I'd have been a millionaire.

'I guess you owe him an apology,' said Floyd.

'I don't owe him nothing,' said the kid.

'It's all right, honey, I've got some green,' said the vamp. 'You can pay me back.' She reached over and plucked his whiskey from the bar and downed it in one go.

The kid sulkily finished off his beer and after a few moments they got up to go. At the door he turned to us.

'I'm going to come back with the police,' he said.

'I don't want to see you in here again,' Floyd said sternly.

They left. The kid was in such a foul mood he'd forgotten all about the rose. I reached over and picked it up. It was Sunday tomorrow. I'd cut the stem down and put it in my buttonhole.

Floyd started pouring me a beer.

'And a whiskey,' I said.

'So how come it wasn't in your pockets?' he asked.

'Because it was under my hat,' I said. I picked up my hat from the bar and plopped it back on my head. The kid's wallet sat there like a big sleeping beetle.

We split the money. I got my bar tab down under a hundred.

The Party Trick

Andrew Newsham

Dervish stood in the garden and flicked the end of his cigarette malevolently onto the roof of the conservatory next door. He hoped it would melt through the plastic and start a fire that would burn their house down. It was a pleasing fantasy but completely unlikely; the roof was an inch thick and a light drizzle was pissing on the world.

It had been a terrible evening and it still wasn't over. Ten or so people remained in his house and were trying to maintain the semblance of a party like a bunch of demented doctors trying to resuscitate a mannequin. It was dead. Everything was dead. It had never really been alive.

Anna had gone home with Steve from accounts, they'd been flirting together all night and she was drunk. They would have sex. The woman he loved would now be sucking the cock of a man who was a weekend warrior with the Territorial Army, a man who didn't read books, a man who was the complete opposite of Dervish.

Steve hadn't even been invited. In fact, half the people who had shown up hadn't been invited. Anna had turned the tenderly proffered invitation to a small dinner party into a free-for-all, a house-warming, a full-on rave. Even the young Chinese couple from up the road had walked in off the street. They didn't speak a word of English and stared like acid freaks in the middle of a flashback at everyone.

Then there was Lesley and Gerald from next door. The old hippies. Gerald was now rolling around on the lounge carpet trying to do a Rubik's Cube with his bare feet. It was his party trick, except of course he couldn't do it. For the past hour he'd been at it, face gurning with the strain, long grey beard dipped in every dish on the buffet table. He didn't look like doing it in a million years. It was this painful stunt that had finally driven Anna and Steve out onto the stairs and then into each other's arms in a shared taxi.

Someone pulled the door open behind him and Dervish was once more confronted with unwanted company. It was Lucy, the fat girl who worked with Anna. She'd taken a shine to him and had been following him around all night with her big cow eyes. Every time he'd tried to talk to Anna she'd appeared with some inane attempt at conversation.

'There you are,' she said. 'I was wondering where you'd got to.'

'Why?'

'Well . . .' She fumbled for a response but the hostility in Dervish's voice threw her off balance. 'Gerald's just completed one side of the cube.'

'Do you really think I give a fuck what that retard does with his feet?'

Her lip wobbled and he knew she was going to cry before she did. What he didn't expect was the slap. She brought her hand around to his face and landed it with a swift crack. In the slow seconds that followed she looked almost as surprised as Dervish.

'Get out,' he said.

She burst into tears and ran back into the house.

It was fucking incredible. Not only would he have to put up with seeing Anna and Steve together at work on Monday morning but now there'd probably be some sort of whispering campaign against him because of this incident as well.

Dervish lit another cigarette and his mind flashed on the moment he'd seen Anna and Steve sat on the stairs holding hands like a pair of loved-up teenagers.

'FUCK,' he shouted into the cold night air.

The ferocity of his desolation took him by surprise. He had perhaps fantasized about being with Anna a little too much, but his utter despair was difficult to understand since he'd always been scornful of love. He found it demeaning that he should be subject to the same gut-churning emotions as fourteen-year-old girls mooning over the latest idiotic pop stars.

The fact was that Anna made his heart skip a beat. If nothing else, she taught him how lonely he was.

It began to rain harder and the water hit the roof like a ripple of applause. Dervish felt his shirt becoming soaked and was just about to go back inside when he noticed an open window on the side of the conservatory next door. Inhaling a last blast from his cigarette, he decided to show Lesley and Gerald a trick of his own. Climbing onto the rim of a concrete flowerpot, he leaned over the fence and threw the burning end of the cigarette through the narrow gap of the open window. It fell down onto a wicker sofa and almost immediately a thin plume of smoke began to stream upwards. Barely a minute later the conservatory was full of orange flames.

Dervish laughed nervously. He was torn between fleeing and running back inside to call the fire brigade. He could always say that he'd just flicked the cigarette in a moment of drunken repose, that it was a bizarre freakish accident. What were the alternatives? He wandered into the middle of the garden and pictured a hotel he knew in Dover. The cliffs were nearby and he could always throw himself off . . .

It was as he stood in thought that he caught sight of the young Chinese couple watching him from the first-floor window of his bedroom. They stared at him, emotionless, hugging each other in the darkness.

Instinctively, Dervish held his hand up in greeting, as if there was nothing wrong at all, as if it was perfectly normal for the host of a party to skulk around setting his guests' houses on fire.

They waved back.

Fucked up the Ass

Andrew Newsham

P*onk*

    I sat thinking at the kitchen table, an open newspaper spread out in front of me unread. It took a while for the sound to break into my consciousness.

Ponk Ponk

It was a strange thumping sound, like a dumb child trying to force a heart-shaped block through a kidney-shaped hole. I got up and went into the garden. My next-door neighbours had hung a new wind chime from the corner of their roof. They'd just moved in a few days ago. There were two of them: an old man with a huge beard and a young guy who could have been his carer or his son, I suppose.

Ponk Ponk

I watched the wooden slats knock together and it suddenly occurred to me that they were meant to be cocks. Each of the chime's wooden teeth was a long penis with a bulbous purple head. They were twisted and deformed, which was why I hadn't noticed them straight away.

'There goes the neighbourhood,' I thought. The words were pronounced in my head in a dull instant, a phrase from some sitcom. You know how it is: short of cognitive therapy costing thousands, you just can't stop yourself.

PONK, KKK

The wind had picked up and blown the thing so hard it couldn't make its regular sound. They were like that, wind chimes: they required a gentle hand. Like the penis, I guess.

I went back inside and picked up the newspaper and read an article about a group of teenagers who had gone missing while trekking around Kashmir. Their parents were worried. Kashmir was a poverty-stricken, war-torn region full of bandits. The kids were probably dead, ripped open like walking pinatas for gifts of cash and Gore-Tex.

The telephone rang. It was my mother instigating our regular Saturday morning call. After the usual pleasantries we ran out of things to say and began talking about Michael, my son. He was the reason I'd moved down here in the first place.

'Don't worry, he doesn't hate you, you're his father . . .' She paused, letting her voice tail off.

I kept quiet; I didn't have anything to say. Fact was that I probably wasn't his actual dad, genetically.

'It's a very difficult age,' she said.

I sometimes find it hard not to imagine my mother as some kind of Wurlitzer Cliché Machine made in the fifties and ordered from an Innovations catalogue and put together in the shed one rainy Sunday afternoon by my father.

'I know,' I sighed.

'You just need to spend more time with him, that's all.'

'That's why I moved down here.'

'But you still hardly see him.'

'I know, but the judge only gave me one weekend in two.'

'But Julia lets you see him more than that.'

'Yes, but it's . . . difficult.' I paused, feeling myself getting tense. We've had this conversation so many times it's difficult not to get pissed off. It's the same shit every day. It's not just my mother: it's everything.

'He needs to spend more time with you, his father.'

'I can't make him see me if he doesn't want to.'

'It's a difficult age,' she says again, and I can almost hear her brain ticking away, picking up on a new line of attack. 'I don't know why he can't go to a normal school anyway? It was good enough before. It's probably putting too much strain on him.'

'Yes,' I say quietly. I picture her face, a simple-minded composite of sad concern.

'You're allowed to take him on holiday for a week, aren't you?'

'Yes . . .'

'It would do you good, it would do you both good. Maybe you could bring him up to visit us, you could go camping, take a boat out on the lakes.'

'I'm broke.'

'I know, but it wouldn't cost that much if you stayed with us.'

'Perhaps.' The move and the divorce had crippled me financially. Then there was the private school Michael was going to now. Somehow Julia had conned me into paying all the fees. It was ridiculous.

'It's a good idea,' said my mother, probing for some firm commitment. She was always full of good ideas. I'm sure she really believed I would be President by now if only I'd followed her advice and yet this is a woman who's not spoken to her sister for five years because of a mislaid tablecloth.

'I'll think about it.'

'You said that last time.'

'I know, but I've not really settled in down here yet . . . things are still up in the air.'

'I'm not going to be here for ever,' she said.

'Don't say things like that.' I switched the phone to my other ear. 'You're immortal.'

She laughed a small, knowing chuckle, then fell silent.

'OK,' I said, 'I'll look into it.'

'Promise?'

'Yes, I promise. Look I've got to go. I'll call you again in the week.'

We said goodbye and put the phone down. After a few moments I realized I'd completely forgotten to ask about my dad. He slipped in the shower a few weeks ago and broke a couple of ribs. I'm surprised she didn't mention it.

I sat at the table some more and watched another delivery van arrive outside, dropping off yet more things for my new neighbours. They seemed to be moving in bit by bit.

I bought this place part furnished so I didn't have to bring anything when I moved down, just my computer and clothes and TV. The rooms were a bit Spartan but there was more than enough furniture for a single man living alone. A washing machine and a new bed for Michael's room were all I'd bought when I got down here.

I got up and made coffee.

Michael's not visiting this weekend. He should be, but a school friend is having a party or something, plus Julia's parents are visiting on Sunday and want to take him out. Julia called in the week and we decided it would be best for Michael to go to the party since he's new in town and has to make friends.

When I say 'we' decided, I mean Julia decided. It's incredible really, the control she still exerts over my life. I've only just started to face up to this.

It was late on Thursday night when she called. Now I've got him next weekend instead.

In a way I'm relieved. Whenever he's here, I always find myself trying to be over-friendly. It's quite tiring.

He's nearly fifteen and has become moody and sullen. I've been told it's quite normal for teenagers. When he was a kid it was so much easier. He used to just like being near me. Now he dresses like one of the kids from Columbine.

Of course, there's nothing in that; you only have to look at the papers to see that serial killers don't wear one kind of uniform.

I went into the back room and switched on my computer. I am a computer programmer for a company called Systems Solutions. Often I could do a lot of work at home. I didn't have any serious deadlines and I didn't have to work weekends, but there was always something I could do.

There was an e-mail from my oldest friend, James. He was an astrophysicist and he sent me photographs of stars and planets at least twice a week. Today there was a picture of a 'new' asteroid that had been spotted in the sky near the edge of our solar system. The message he sent with the picture said: 'Did you know that your hair is full of tiny meteorites?'

'Yes, that's why I always wear a shower cap,' I wrote back.

Actually, I didn't know that there were loads of tiny bits of space dust in my hair. It made sense though, somehow. It was only air and space above us; something had to get through.

I started some work I was doing for an insurance firm who wanted to move their accounts on-line.

It was gone six when the doorbell rang. I'd lost track of time. I went to the door and found one of my new neighbours waiting on the step.

'Hi there,' he said. 'I'm Jay.' He was holding a large cardboard box, which he put down on the step, and offered me his hand. We shook and he held on a fraction longer than was necessary.

'I've just moved in next door,' he said, locking his eyes on mine with a glittering, flirtatious stare.

'David,' I said.

'Nice smooth hands,' he said. 'With hands like that you could get lucky . . .'

I was surprised and stuck for words. I wasn't used to people coming to my door and flirting with me, especially men. Not that I'm homophobic. To be honest, I'm not really a very sexual person. It just doesn't appeal to me; it all seems rather foolish, all that thrusting for so little reward. My sex life amounts to an occasional wank over pictures on the Internet of naked women with large breasts.

This was the first time a man had ever come on to me.

'That's why I'm here,' he continued, 'to see if you want to be lucky.' Jay smiled. I'm not sure but I might have blushed.

He bent down and grabbed the box. 'It's a lucky dip, for charity.' He opened the cardboard flaps revealing a huge mound of Styrofoam packing pieces.

'Oh, I see,' I said.

'It's ten bucks a go but the prizes are really out of this world!'

'Ten bucks, well I don't know if I have any cash on me at the moment.' I pulled my wallet out of my pocket. I hoped I wouldn't have more than a couple of dollars and then I could get out of it.

I opened my wallet and there was a single twenty-dollar bill sticking up from inside. Jay's eyes lit up. I looked behind it hoping to find something smaller, but it was on its own.

'Do you have change?' I asked.

'No,' he said and quickly reached forward and took the twenty from my hand. 'But seeing as you're so cute, I'll let you have three goes for the price of two.'

I gasped as he tucked the note away in his shirt pocket and held up the box to me.

'Go on,' he said. 'I just know you're going to be lucky.'

I knew that now was the time to get my money back and call the whole thing to a halt. Instead I found myself putting my hand into the box.

'You're feeling for envelopes,' he said.

I rooted around and Styrofoam bits jumped and bobbled out of the box onto the doorstep. I felt an envelope and pulled it out.

'Which charity is it for?' I asked.

'MUFTI. They're based downtown. They work with young kids, trying to get them off the streets.' He paused before adding defiantly, 'Young male prostitutes actually.'

'Great,' I muttered. I opened the envelope. I'd never heard of MUFTI before but then why would I have done?

I pulled out a slip of paper, printed on it were the words: 'Sorry, you have not won this time.' I showed it to Jay.

'Oh well, I'm sure you'll get lucky this time.'

I reached back into the box and pulled out another envelope.

'Fingers crossed!' cried Jay.

Inside was another slip of paper: 'Sorry, you have not won this time.'

'I don't believe it!' he said. 'That's just unreal. Go on, try again; you must win something.'

'What are the prizes?'

'There's all sorts: a coffee machine, some wind chimes, a bottle of wine. The top prize is a beauty treatment and haircut at Raphael's!'

My heart sank. Wind chimes.

I pulled out another envelope. This time the slip read: 'Congratulations, you have won a prize!'

Jay cheered and dropped the box to the step. 'Hooray for David!' He jumped forward and hugged me.

'Thanks, so what have I won?' The bottle of wine would be something, not twenty dollars of something, but something.

'You've won one of our special prizes, not one of the top ones, but it'll be good nevertheless. And of course you've also helped a terribly mixed-up kid.'

I should have felt good about the charity donation, but

I just felt cheated. What was it again? Male prostitutes? Did they really deserve my twenty? Some people deliberately hurt themselves all the time. They go in for all kinds of seedy self-destruction. Maybe Jay was a rent boy. The way he flirted and held my hand and pouted in his skintight leather top all fitted.

'I haven't got your prize with me but I can drop it off tomorrow. Unless you'd like to collect it now – you can go next door and wake Frank up.'

'Frank?'

'Yes, he's my partner. He sleeps a lot in the afternoon, it's his new medication.'

I'd seen Jay a few times when the delivery vans came. There was also the old guy in the wheelchair. He was about thirty or forty years older than Jay. He had a huge beard and whenever he went out he wore a black leather peaked cap.

'He's very depressed,' continued Jay, 'the poor love. The doctor keeps trying him on all sorts of stuff but none of it works. He can walk, that's the thing, the doctors say it's all in his head.' He paused and let the point sink in. 'He's a great talent, though, a real artist.'

'What does he do?'

'He was a famous poet in the seventies, used to work with Ginsberg, but now he's more tactile . . . in the arts, I mean, pottery, painting. He even makes wind chimes. You'll have to pop by, he loves meeting new people.'

'Right,' I said half-heartedly.

Jay picked up his box and started to walk back down the drive. 'Must dash, so many more lucky people on this street, I can feel it.'

'Bye.' I stepped back into the house and closed the door.

I knew with certainty that I had been taken. I had paid twenty bucks for a penis wind chime.

*

It was the story of my whole life. At school I'd been bullied. My mother never let up, always criticizing everything. When I met Julia I thought things had changed but once the honeymoon was over it was all downhill. We had Michael almost immediately because she was 'desperate for children' and yet we'd had no more together. I sold my computer business because she wanted a bigger house. Then she wanted a divorce. I couldn't see why but she always got her own way. Result, she took half of everything I owned and moved to Florida with her new lover. I had moved down here just to be near Michael. I was a doormat, had been all my life. Now all people had to do was turn up and I'd give them my money.

I went upstairs and took the gun out of the drawer in my bedside table. It was loaded. I sat down on the edge of the bed and weighed it in my hands. I looked up into the bedroom mirror. Impulsively I placed the gun to my head. That's the thing about guns, what else are you supposed to do with them? They carry a certain inbuilt agenda – like pianos in old school halls, someone was always lifting the lid and pressing a few keys. I clenched my teeth and grimaced at myself.

'Just do it, you fucking pussy!'

My finger rested on the trigger. One tiny little bit of pressure and that would be it. I imagined Julia at my funeral. She would be crying, not through sorrow; just to be the centre of attention. I lowered the gun and put it back in the drawer. I wouldn't give her the satisfaction.

I went back downstairs and made some coffee and got to thinking about what I could do to get some more money. Nothing came to mind except going into business with Frank and Jay selling his penis wind chimes door-to-door at ten per cent commission. At least I probably wouldn't have to shoot myself. There'd be plenty of people happy to do it for me.

I went back to my computer, clicked onto the Internet and sent James a message: 'I've just been taken for twenty bucks by the fags next door.' I waited a few minutes. He's always on-line; he works constantly. I think the only time he's away from his screen is when he gives lectures.

No reply. It was Saturday night after all. Maybe he'd finally gone out and got a life.

I did some of my own work for about an hour and there was still no reply so I took some sleeping pills and went to bed.

At around two a.m. I was woken by shouting from next door. Something was thrown. Something smashed, it sounded like a patio door. I got up and looked out into the garden. Frank appeared, out of his wheelchair. He walked around the pool in their garden, talking wildly into a mobile phone. He kicked a sun lounger into the water and went back inside. After a while I heard another smash and then I fell back to sleep.

At six a.m. I was woken again. This time the argument was out the front of the house. Frank and Jay were arguing on their lawn over money. There was a taxi waiting. Frank was back in his wheelchair. Eventually Frank paid the taxi. Jay wandered inside, laughing. He was drunk.

I couldn't get back to sleep so I got up and cleaned the kitchen. At the computer I found a reply from James: 'Twenty bucks? You're worth more than that, twenty-two at least.'

I typed back, 'Thanks. My ass hurts.'

Like the day before there was no instant response so I started to do some work. I wasn't paid extra for working on Sundays but in the long run my efforts would pay off. I'd soon become indispensable to the company. That was the theory anyway, like being nice and faithful to your wife for seven years and then getting screwed in the divorce courts.

At around four p.m. the doorbell went. I ignored it; it was probably Jay with my 'prize'. He pressed the bell three times, leaning on it for a good twenty seconds each time, before he gave up. He probably knew I was home. Tough shit.

Later, I got another e-mail from James. It was headed: 'Big News Old Chum!'

> I'm getting married! No joke. Her name's Erika. She's a German physicist. We've been working together for the past couple of months and it's just incredible. You might think we're rushing things but it's so good, it feels so right. We think the same. We're going to tie the knot next weekend in Las Vegas. I know it's a bit short notice but it would be great if you could make it. What do you think?

My first feeling was disbelief and then amazement and then disbelief again and then everything hardened into envy. The happiness I knew I should have felt for him sounded like a recorded message of an emotion, hollowed out by my own self-pity.

At college he hadn't even been able to talk to girls, any girls, even the nervous mouse-like ones who were with us in the science department. Time flies. We were both now fast approaching forty. I was at the end of one marriage and he was at the start of another.

'Wow. Congratulations!!!' I wrote back.

He replied after a few moments. 'So you'll come?'

My first thoughts were about the cost and then I remembered I had Michael visiting. 'I've got my son staying over next weekend,' I typed back.

'So bring him. I'm sure he'll love Vegas, every young boy's dream!'

He was right: Michael would love Las Vegas, even though his teenage cool would demand that he didn't show it. The simple fact was that I just didn't have the cash.

Several minutes went by and I hadn't replied when he sent another message: 'I've got to go and meet Erika now, so much to sort out, I'll call you tonight!'

I sat back and read the series of messages over again. After a while the screen-saver kicked in. I started to search the Internet for hotels in Vegas. Like everyone, I'd heard about free rooms that casinos give out in the hope you'll spend three times as much gambling. A free room would be a start.

I'd have to postpone Michael's visit to the weekend after.

It would be good to take him along but Julia would never agree. Not out of any concern about his welfare, just on principle. She hates the idea of us doing great things together. She's not anti-gambling but could concoct an argument against it at a moment's notice.

On-line, I found some cheap Vegas rooms, but no complimentary ones. Flights were a couple of hundred dollars. I checked my bank account. I was overdrawn. There was just no way I could afford it. I checked a few loan companies.

The doorbell went again. I was relieved to get away from the interest rates flickering on the screen.

I opened the door expecting Jay, but was greeted by an old woman with a scowling face and a thin bird-like neck around which hung a large silver crucifix.

'Hello, Mr Glover, I'm so glad you're home,' she said without sounding like she was glad I was home or anywhere. 'I'm Beverley Spangol of the West Park residents' association.'

'Hi,' I said. On the doorstep at my feet was a brown paper bag. I bent down and picked it up.

'I'm sorry I haven't been round sooner but I normally leave it to Mr Thomas to say hello to our bachelors when they arrive. He's a good man but a little forgetful.'

'I wasn't aware there was a residents' association.'

'Well, I think it would be rather remiss if there wasn't.'

She stared at me with a strange intensity. I dropped my eyes into the bag. There were two items, a square box and a plastic bottle. I looked up at her and smiled.

She didn't smile back. 'It is only by banding together that we can protect our homes from attack, safeguard our souls and fight the constant onslaught of poisonous evil.'

'I'm sorry?'

'Evil, Mr Glover, is all around us. It waits to seduce us from the path of righteousness and comes at us in all forms.'

'I don't really believe in any organized religion, I'm afraid,' I said tentatively.

She grabbed my arm. 'Then you are in mortal danger, Mr Glover. The eternal quality of your soul is at stake.'

I shrugged. She dropped her hand.

'Of course that is up to you. The Lord knows all and has plans for everyone.'

'I'm sorry, I'm really rather busy . . .' I said as politely as possible and began to close the door.

'But, Mr Glover, you must have seen with your own eyes that there is trouble brewing!'

I looked at her blankly.

She glanced over her shoulder and then stepped in close. 'Your neighbours,' she hissed.

'There was a bit of noise last night but I'm sure it's just an isolated incident.'

'Men coming and going at all hours, sodomy perpetrated near children, obscene garden ornaments . . .' As she spoke the veins stood out on her neck and she clasped her crucifix in her hands.

'I'm sorry, I've got to go,' I said, closing the door. She said something else but I didn't hear it right. It sounded like a Bible quote. I walked down the corridor towards the kitchen. She continued to speak through the door.

'Love Thy Neighbour,' I shouted.

After a while she gave up and walked away.

My 'prizes' turned out to be bottle of Golden Girl Anal Lubricant and a Wanky Wanky Wind Chime identical to the one outside. Attached to the box was a note: 'David, I said you were lucky! Frank & Jay xxxx'

I was sure the Bible told us to 'love thy neighbour' but I doubt even the maddest fundamentalists would take it as an instruction to go next door and fuck them up the ass.

I went to the kitchen and put my prizes on the table and set about making some dinner. Afterwards I had a shower with the radio turned up loud and then I took some sleeping pills and went to bed. I told myself it would all look different in the morning. I would ask my boss for an advance on my wage.

That night I dreamt I was in Las Vegas with Michael. I was dressed in rags and losing heavily at a game that looked like solitaire. Across the floor Michael was winning. He was older than fifteen. Everyone loved him. I tried to talk to him but some heavy-set security men stepped in and pushed me away. I got lost in a maze of corridors and when I finally found my room a naked old man with painted eyes was in my bed. He looked like my father.

The next few days passed in a blur. I was busy at work and as it turned out my boss was away all week on holiday so there was no chance of an advance before the weekend.

It was Wednesday night before James rang and I still hadn't sorted any money out for the trip. I hadn't even called Michael to postpone his visit. It was looking more and more unlikely that I would go, but James was so happy and carefree that it was hard to tell him about my troubles and so I let him believe that I would be in Vegas, come what may. In the back of my mind there was still a flicker of hope.

When I got home from work the next night I made the call. As usual, Brad was the first to the phone. It was, after all, his house. He was Julia's lover. That was fine but he was always so perky, so chipper. It got on my nerves. He spoke to me as if I was a clown, the butt of an immense joke.

'Hi, is Michael in?' I asked.

'David! How's it going, you got used to the traffic system yet?' When I first moved here it took me a while to get used to the one-way nightmare of the city centre and on one occasion, with Michael in the car, I made a wrong turn and nearly caused a pile-up. Brad seemed to get some kind of kick out of bringing it up every time we spoke.

'I'm fine,' I said, cutting any further chatter short with an unfriendly silence. He laughed gently and put the phone down.

Even though I'd asked for Michael it was no surprise when Julia came on the phone. The boy was almost fifteen and yet his mother watched and monitored his every interaction with me.

'What is it, David?' she asked curtly. She was a legal secretary. I think it burned her a bit that she wasn't an actual lawyer but she hadn't been able to get through college because she couldn't let go of cock for long enough to pick up a book. At least that's how I think it was. When we first separated I was in pieces. I had a lot of time on my hands. I did some research on how she was before she got her claws into me.

'Hi, Julia, how are you?' I asked.

'Great, I've lost two pounds, I'm fitter than I've ever been, but let's cut the crap. Brad's taking me out tonight and I want to look my best.'

'Well, actually I wanted to talk to Michael.'

'He's not in but I'll tell him you called.' She went to put the phone down.

I was ready for it, however, and caught her just in time. 'Wait,' I said, 'I've got something I need to talk about.'

She sighed. 'Make it quick.'

'You remember my friend James? He's the astronomer in California.'

'No.'

'He's my oldest friend. He came to our wedding.'

'Whatever.' She hated being reminded of our marriage. She described it in court as 'seven years in hell'. This was a bit strong but she had talked me into a quick divorce for the good of Michael and so I played the bad guy. It was a stupid mistake and one I regret, like losing your queen at the start of a game of chess. The idea had been that she would continue to be my 'friend' and allow unchecked access to Michael but as the years went by she started to believe all that was said in court, even though I'd been a devoted husband and she was the one who'd been screwing around.

'He's getting married, it's a total whirlwind romance, kind of like how ours was.'

'Great, so what do you want me to do?'

'The wedding is this weekend, in Las Vegas . . .'

'No way, David. It's absolutely out of the question.'

'What, I . . .'

'You are not taking my son to that city. He's at a very impressionable age.'

'I know, I'm not going to take him, I was just going to postpone his visit for another week.'

'But it was already put back from last weekend.'

'That was you, you called me last week, remember?' I said firmly.

'Don't raise your voice at me!'

'I didn't raise my voice,' I said, raising my voice. There was a long pause. I counted to five calmly in my head.

'It's a bit late to go changing the plans, David. I'm sure

Michael doesn't like all this. He hasn't seen you in over a month. You can't just choose to be his dad when it suits you.'

'No, I can only be his dad when it suits *you*.'

'Whatever.' She laughed. 'Look, I'm sorry but you have to have him this weekend because you're not the only one with plans.'

'What?'

'Brad's taking me to the Keys. We've got a boat with some friends, it's been planned for weeks.'

'Why do I always have to back down, Julia? Why won't you do something for me?'

She cut me off. I called her straight back. It rang seven or eight times before Brad answered.

'Hi,' he said brightly.

'Can you just put Julia back on, Brad?'

'She doesn't want to talk to you right now, man. She's getting ready and we're going to be late.'

'*Just put her on the goddamn phone.*'

The line went dead again. I threw the phone across the room.

THE BITCH THE FUCKING BITCH FUCK FUCK FUCK.

My mind lit on the gun in the drawer upstairs and I stalked around the house from room to room imagining trailing Brad and Julia to some fancy restaurant and shooting them both in the face.

A few hours later and I'd managed to calm down. The adrenalin rush had made me really tired and I collapsed into bed.

That night I was woken at about twelve by the sound of partying from next door. I looked out of my window. Several men were skinny-dipping and messing around in the pool. One of them was Frank. They had taken a ghettoblaster outside and were singing along to Dolly Parton.

'Jolene, Jolene, Jolene, *Jolene*!' they howled like alley cats.

I took out my gun, cleaned it and then practised aiming at them. I wasn't the only person to be disturbed because the police turned up a few moments later, bathing the front of the house in flickering blue light. The police went straight round the back to the garden and received a chorus of wolf whistles from the men in the pool as if they were the Village People. It was totally the wrong thing to do. The music was switched off. The police took Frank away. A group of the partygoers gathered around Jay who was sobbing on a sun lounger. It was pure street theatre. I laughed and felt considerably better.

In the post the next day I got a letter from Michael's school. It said how his 'absences' were having a bad effect on his grades and how extra tuition would be required if he was going to stand a chance of not being held back a year. The extra tuition was offered at a premium of one hundred dollars an hour.

I read the line again about 'absences having a bad effect on his grades'. I drove to work wondering just what the fuck was going on. After a while I started to wonder if I could turn the information to my advantage.

I left work early and when I got home I found the front door unlocked. There was no sign of a break-in. I walked cautiously to the kitchen and immediately met Michael's gaze as he sat facing the door. I'd forgotten he had a key. Sun streamed though the window and made his blond hair glow. He was the spitting image of his mother and if it wasn't for the black Marilyn Manson T-shirt he wore I would have sworn he was in fact her little sister.

'Oh it's you,' I said.

'Mum dropped me off, they're going sailing,' he said, looking sad.

'Great.' I took off my jacket and slung it over one of the chairs. In his hands I saw that he was fiddling about with the bottle of anal lube. I must have left it on the table. Next to it sat the Wanky Wanky Wind Chime. A dozen thoughts crossed my mind. I didn't know if he even knew the facts of life or had a girlfriend or anything. Would he think I was gay? Whatever he thought, I was sure it would give Brad and Julia a good laugh.

I filled the kettle. 'You want a drink?'

'No,' he said.

Ponk Ponk

The wind had picked up outside.

I looked at Michael sitting stiffly in his chair. I didn't know what to say. Suddenly, he started crying. I edged up to him awkwardly and put my arms round him.

'But you're not my real dad,' he said through the tears.

'I know,' I said.

'So why do you put up with her?'

'I don't know.'

Ponk Ponk

My mind slid easily to the gun in the drawer.

Mick Scully

MICK SCULLY lives in Birmingham. 'Little Moscow', his first short story in the Little Moscow series, was published in the Tindal Street Press anthology *Birmingham Noir* in 2002. Mick is currently completing *The Heart of St Agnes*, a literary crime novel set in Amsterdam, Prague and Vietnam.

Abstract
Mick Scully

Sure. Murders happen in Birmingham, like everywhere. Hamid knew this. But it isn't every day you see a man hanging from a lamp-post, his spectacles shattered three feet beneath his shoes. In other places, yes.

And in the afternoon too. Long after noon. Four p.m. to be precise. It was November, and that grey-orange light – so familiar in England at that time of day, at that time of year – suffused the decaying street, gracing the boarded-up houses and broken gates with an undeserved romanticism.

When Hamid saw him, hanging simply and still, like a pendant, he knew he would never have to work in Durscher's Eight till Late Convenience Store again. The sweeping and packing, the grovelling, were over.

The hanging man was a gift, and Hamid knew he was a gift meant for him. He shinned the lamp-post to the point where he could lean across and unravel the rope. The carcass fell in a heap.

It had been his intention to use the rope to drag the dead man into the cover of a doorway, or down that passage between two derelict houses. But that would ruin the clothes. And they were clothes of such good quality. Fashionable.

He had risked much in his life. And for what? Well, he was here. What was one more risk? He heard the hum of traffic from the nearby motorway. One impatient driver seeking a shortcut and he was undone.

He raised the dead man to a sitting position, lolling against the lamp-post. He was young, about thirty. A similar age to Hamid. But even in death the face contained the remains of a youth Hamid felt he'd never had. He's a little heavier than me, Hamid judged, but that won't matter. And he started to strip the corpse.

For those who have long given up hope of fortune smiling upon them, when luck arrives it is accepted circumspectly, without shock or celebration. So, when Hamid felt the weight of the jacket and discovered the wallet with its credit cards and wad of notes, when he heard the rattle of keys in the trouser pocket, he wasn't surprised; it was as if he were receiving his due.

For Hamid, it was a pleasure to remove his own clothes. Even here in the cold, darkening street. To feel the cheap, warm garments, stiffened by sweat, fall away from him into a heap at his feet. Then to bend slowly to the expensive clothing resting in the dead man's lap. The shirt first. Then shorts. Striped. He didn't check to see if they were stained. It was possible. But he didn't look. Blood. Piss. Shit. He didn't care. If they were, then he would carry the relic of his benefactor with him. The trousers were looser than he would have liked, but he would get a belt.

The touch of the sweater. Soft as a woman. He stroked it before taking possession of it. Cashmere.

When all of the dead man's clothes were upon Hamid's back, he picked up the shattered spectacles and, folding them, placed them carefully in the top pocket of his jacket. Something else was in there too. Four condoms. Hamid smiled. His first smile for a long time. Then he stooped to the rags beside the dead man and started to dress him.

Getting him back up the lamp-post was more difficult than releasing him. After all that hauling and tying of knots, the rope had scoured strips of skin from his fingers and palms.

Inside the wallet, tucked behind banknotes, a postcard reminded Mr Martin Burrows of Flat 46 St Nicholas Towers, Bell Tower Grove, Edgbaston, Birmingham, that he should visit his dentist on 2nd December. Hamid read the dead man's address again.

There was purple in the sky, indicating imminent darkness, when Hamid started to make his way towards Edgbaston. He listened to his footsteps upon the pavement. Good leather shoes make a satisfying sound. Better than the humiliating slap of worn rubber from his trainers which had echoed his every step for months now.

As he walked, Hamid was aware that he knew not what he might have to confront upon his arrival. A wife. A family. An elderly mother, perhaps. It didn't matter. His destiny was held in the elegant click of his shoes.

He thought he knew the way to Edgbaston. He was sure he did. First, make for the city centre. Down to the busy streets. Moving against the traffic, which nosed in follow-my-leader formation, as if attempting to escape a catastrophe, or a war zone. To escape. A creeping trail of paired lights. Moving minutely. Stopping. Moving again. He had more speed than they did. He was unafraid of catastrophes or war zones. He had met these devils before. His stride lengthened. There is always a cave, a hollow tree. There is. Always. I need no map. Shoes as expensive as these know where to go.

He stood, for a moment, held by his reflection in the large glass doors of St Nicholas Towers. I am a new man. Within his own reflection he saw the lights of the apartment blocks behind him. The city's expensive streets were contained within his shadow on the glass. Inside, a brass plate beside the elevator revealed his apartment was on the fifth floor. The elevator zoomed him soundlessly to it.

He placed the key in the lock and turned. There was no hesitation. No fear. Nothing to be gained by pause. But there was a tension within his limbs – a coil, ready to spring if action was required. The feeling pleased him. It was the closest he had come to power in a long time. He felt strong again.

The apartment was in empty darkness. Beyond, he recognized a change in the quality of that darkness as a door stood ajar at the end of the hallway. Banging the door behind him, he marched fowards. This was the lounge. The sitting room. A Venetian blind produced stripes of light and lesser darkness against a large window. He found a couch upon which to sit. This was good. He had come a long way. It was time to sit down and rest. The lights of the city outside sparkled between the slats of the blind.

As he sat at ease on the comfortable couch the shapes in the darkness became distinct. A chair over there. A lamp here beside him at the end of the couch.

Of course, such darkness prompted memories. The darkness of his long journey to this country. The sound of the lorry's drone returned to his ears. That constant, relentless drone, which continued for suffocating hour after hour. There were eight of them. Jammed into the small compartment. Lying flat out. No one spoke. Just the drone of the engine. The stench of themselves. The rhythm of the wheels.

But the blackness was a joke. There were a lot of jokes. Release. That word could make him laugh. Release from his country, which had sunk into darkness. Release from the lorry into the dark days that followed. The tenement hovel they shared. The long hours of drudgery in Durscher's Eight till Late Convenience Store. Unpacking. Stacking. Sweeping. Cleaning. For almost nothing. It was a joke and his pain was the knowledge that it was the end of the road, there was no way out. 'Complain if you wish,' Durscher jeered. 'You'll get not a penny more, you bastards. You're lucky to be here.' He lifted a fat finger and waved it at them in warning. 'Remember. One word from me to the right people, and you'll be in a cell. Then back home.' So day followed day like the turning of a millwheel.

'But it is finished,' Hamid whispered to himself. 'Hanging from a lamp-post in the dark.'

But when the darkness eventually became intolerable, as darkness does, Hamid reached out and flicked a switch. Instantly the room filled with yellow gloom, a mocking reminder of the bright days he had once known. But he saw there were other lamps in the room and went to them one by one, increasing the light with each flick of a switch; like turning up the sun.

'This is a rich man's apartment,' Hamid muttered as he looked around the room. Large and comfortable. There were pictures in the room that were images of nothing – abstract is what they are called. Their jangled colours spoke of chaos and confusion, and it was right they should be here in such a modern room.

In the kitchen a stark striplight made him blink. Such a kitchen. Empty and full at the same time. Smooth steel surfaces reflecting the brightness. There were no handles, but indentations. Perfect finger spaces in the shining flatness. Hamid rested a finger in one and pressed. The door clicked and swung open on a cupboard full of more metal. Pots. Pans. Machines. Another depression produced a drawer of cutlery, another the refrigerator. It held a plate covered in foil. Hamid peeled it back, revealing pink fish. Fresh. Two pieces. There were bottles of beer in there too. Lots of them.

Back to the lounge. There were no books. Racks of CDs. A large television. A pile of magazines. But no books. Not even a Bible. And certainly no Koran. Hamid looked at the formless rioting colours of the pictures again.

He went into the bedroom. A double bed. This will provide me with great comfort tonight, he thought, and was about to praise God for the blessing bestowed upon him – but he did not, could not. The wheels had turned endlessly in the darkness, and here he was in the light. Electric light.

He returned to the kitchen where even the floor shone. The gleam of temple tiles. He pressed his finger into the depressions of the disguised cupboards. One contained bottles of wine. I will drink alcohol tonight in my new home, he thought. He found a corkscrew, large and viciously dangerous, but changed his mind. I will drink beer, as Englishmen do. And he selected a bottle from the refrigerator.

Two pieces of pink fish. He re-covered them. Vaguely, they worried him. The beer was called Budweiser. The label proclaimed it 'The King of Beers'. He had seen bottles of beer like this in Durscher's Eight till Late Convenience Store. There was a large glass-fronted fridge that hummed loudly at the back of the shop, filled with different beers, Budweiser prominent among them.

The beer was gassy and very cold. It had little flavour. But after the first gulp it was easy to drink.

Hamid sat on the polished wooden floor of the lounge flicking through CDs. So many of them. Who had time to listen to so much music? Lots of pop bands he had never heard of. Then some classical music. This he was more familiar with. He selected one. Mozart's *Clarinet Concerto*. A picture of a castle wreathed in mist on the cover. Through trial and error he discovered how to use the remote control and when the music took possession of the room it pleased him.

He took a second beer and went to the window. It was raining now. A silly indecisive rain. The weather here is like the people, without passion or determination, he thought. The lights of Birmingham were smeared like an abstract painting into white and gold streaks by the weak indecisive rain.

The phone rang. Tension coiled in him again. Four rings. Five. Decisively he moved towards it. But a voice halted him. 'This is Martin. I can't take your call right now. Sorry.' The voice of the dead man. 'But leave a message after the tone and I'll get back to you just as soon as I can.'

After a pause, another voice. A man's. 'Martin? Are you there? I thought you'd've been back ages ago. Are you there? I wanted to know how it went. No. You're not there, are you? I'm coming over anyway. See you.' A click, followed by a tone that repeated and repeated. A button on the phone shone yellow. And the tone repeated over and over. It was impossible to ignore. It was destroying the Mozart.

Hamid stooped beside the phone and pressed the yellow button. The phone clicked, then, 'Martin. You greedy, cheatin' bastard.' Hamid recognized the tones of a Birmingham accent. He recognized, too, the anger and hostility in the voice. He had met these things before. 'How the fuck did you think you could get away with a stunt like this? You dozy bastard. Listen. Be at the Moscow at two. And bring the stuff with you. And no tricky business. Got that?'

Then a woman's voice: 'You were called today at ten seventeen a.m. The caller withheld their number.' The message from the young man who was coming over anyway repeated, before the woman's voice announced tersely 'End of messages.' Then there was only Mozart.

Hamid went to the kitchen. He selected the largest, sharpest knife he could find. 'I will have to kill him when he arrives,' he said. A statement of fact unaccompanied by any sentiment.

In just a couple of hours Hamid had taken occupancy of Martin's life. He was not going to lose it easily. This is the way things are done. He had never killed before, but he had thought about it many times. It is a pity it is not

Durscher, he thought, as he laid the knife behind a cushion and went again to the window. In the watery light he saw the soldiers drag his father and his brother from the house, heard the shots. He heard the screams of his wife and the hungry grunts and chortles of the soldiers. 'I have come so far,' he confided to the city. 'I can do whatever I have to do. I belong to you now.' And once again he had to quell the desire to thank God and to pray. Instead he looked out again onto the weeping city and, as he slurped his beer, the impulse disappeared. Hamid's breath on the glass obscured the lights and he wiped it away to retrieve them.

He replayed the CD as he sat waiting. I am a warrior. I will kill as a warrior. I am fighting for the lights out there. He turned off the lamps and, when the music died, silence and darkness regained the room.

He knew that he had changed. In these clothes he wanted what he had previously despised. This comfortable room. The aggressive kitchen. What else was there now but the gleam of possessions and power? I am here. And his toes stretched in his expensive leather shoes.

When the key turned in the lock he was fully coiled. He was the soldier in the hills ready to rain down in terror. He heard the rush of movement through the hallway, but did not move or turn his head until the light sprang on.

The woman stood frozen in the doorway, and Hamid thought of the two pieces of pink fish waiting in the refrigerator. Of course.

'What? Who are you?' The voice husky with surprise. 'What are you doing here? Where's Martin?' She was pretty. Blond hair, glittering as it caught the light. Tall, and thin. Her pink skirt was very short and she wore a furry jacket. Grey.

He rose. He would have to move quickly. The man who was coming over anyway would be here soon. I will have to kill twice tonight. So be it. The words came easily to his mind, and as he heard them he was convinced by them. Surely she would be too. 'I am to stay here. For a day or two. I am a friend of Martin's. He said he was taking some stuff. He didn't know when he would be back.'

She seemed to be accepting this. She looked him up and down. He felt calm. She might be afraid. He was not. He was a warrior.

Then, suddenly, a cry. 'Why the fuck are you wearing his sweater?'

Still he was unperturbed, though he did not like a woman swearing like this. But. Maybe. This will make it easier. 'I have nothing. He has given me clothes to wear. He has done much for me.'

Cautiously she came further in to the room. 'Where is he?'

What could he say? 'I know only that he has taken the stuff to the place. The Moscow. To meet with the man he has cheated.'

There was a slight gasp. She was weighing the words. They had not been wrong. But Hamid knew they were only purchasing him a little time. They were a currency he was not rich in. Soon she would want more. So, he thought, it will be as it must be.

He was smiling confidently as he sat down. She, unsure what to do, turned towards the hallway, hesitated, then turned back into the room. Hamid's hand rested on the cushion. He tapped it. His composure reassured her and she took the gesture as an invitation to sit beside him, which she did. Closer than he expected. His nostrils filled with her perfume.

He lifted the bottle of beer towards her. She smiled as she took it, but he did not like the way she guzzled it back. 'Thanks.' She leaned further back, stretching out her long legs. It was already decided. His erection hurt as it forced itself against the fabric of his pants. He would have her. Two or three times. At least once in the clean bed where he could stretch out above her, here on the couch, on the floor, perhaps across that low table over there. On the magazines.

She was pretty. Painted pretty, but pretty nonetheless.

Her makeup was very heavy. Her lips, pink and glossy. The light reflected in her dark eyes. A tiny lamp in each. He let his knee push against hers, and she did not object. 'Has Martin told you about me?'

'Yes.' He lifted the knife from behind the cushion and leaned towards her.

'Fucking Jesus!' Such profanity. She should not speak like this. Her shiny pink mouth was curved in shock. He liked the look of her face like this. She made to cry out as he moved further towards her, but no sound came. Her eyes darted. She was young and pretty, but wore too much makeup. She was breathing deeply, and her skirt was far up her legs. She was frightened but she would relax, he knew it. He could do this for her.

He placed his hand upon her knee, which held steady rather than jerking in alarm. A slight push opened the legs. No resistance. Easy. He knew what he was going to do and pleasure was dripping through him. She averted her eyes – she could not look the enemy in the eye at her moment of surrender. His hand travelled smoothly up the thigh heading for the crotch.

His fingers touched the satin of her pants. He trembled. But then – confusion. A hard obstruction. A shocked realization whipped his hand back, and in that moment a fist reared up beneath his hand, sending the knife hurtling across the room while a punch to the side of his face knocked him from the couch to sprawl upon the floor. With a clatter the knife lodged within the slats of the

Venetian blind. She was up and away, high heels kicked to fly across the room. Vaulting the arm of the couch, she made for the door.

Hamid sat blinking on the floor. The feel of hard cock beneath the sweet satin still on his fingers, the knife jangling in the blinds. He heard a door bang.

Waiting for the room to right itself, he stroked his jaw where the blow had landed, then rose, steadying himself against the couch, and made his way towards the window to retrieve his knife. He would return it to the kitchen. Then he would leave.

He tugged at the jammed knife and the blind pulled away from its fixing and jangled to the floor, exposing the city of glinting lights. Their patterns merely hinted at shape – a galaxy of smeary twinkles and glints in the rain. Then her reflection reared up behind him. He turned. She jabbed the corkscrew towards him.

The battle was over. He knew it. He came from a place of certainty, a land of rocks and stones and mountains. Here was the chaos of the abstract; a map in turmoil. She was part of this. He was not. He could not win.

The defeat lay within his dull eyes. She knew, he thought. Understood that for her the threat was gone. She held the power now; she poked the corkscrew at him as if it were a gun. 'Sit down. There. Now, tell me what's happening.'

It was an impossible command. He didn't have enough words. But he told her what he knew as well as he could.

She was pressing towards him. Listening hard. But there was more. He felt her attention like body weight upon him.

He knew now that he was not to be ripped by the curled metal spike she held. She would not gouge deep holes in his flesh, like those made by bullets, through which his blood would leak to extinction.

But he understood, too, by her breath on his face and

the tilt of her body towards him, the look in her eyes, hungry as his people, that there was a price to pay. He had stumbled. Tumbled. He had fallen. She would exact her price. And he would pay it. Gladly, perhaps. For this is the way things are done here.

He could see her cleavage. Real breasts. Flesh. She had real breasts and a cock. What type of creature is this?

Outside the rain was fierce now. Decisive. It pounded the window viciously, obliterating all but the most eloquent squiggles and daubs.

He had been taken, so obediently he followed her to the bed. It would not be so bad. No. There were those of his countrymen who had chosen a similar path in order to survive, and prospered. It was cash in the pocket for them.

He walked behind her. This was some trust. A compliment from the conqueror. He felt some power returning. He would do it well. He was here. It was his destiny.

In the bedroom he made himself look, watch. The pink skirt fell. He saw the bulge of the satin pants. Pink too. 'Leave them on,' he said. The hips were fine, and the painted face so very pretty.

In bed she leaned across him. He could feel her cock, hard against his thigh, as she reached for the lamp. 'No. Leave it on,' he said.

'Yes, Martin. If that's what you want,' she replied.

Yes, Martin. It is the price we pay. The abstract confusion. But it is OK. And he moved himself on top of her, his cock pressing on hers, and closed his eyes. Tomorrow I will shave my beard. I will cut my hair, he thought.

There came a moment while he was in her, looking down at the pimples on her back, when everything became clear. He had turned his eyes towards the lamp, its light blurring his vision, so that he saw again the pictures in the lounge, his pictures now, the abstracts. He understood that such art could only come from lands where there exists endless electricity, false light, where things collide in it, brutally, but where it is possible to survive such collisions.

Secret Smile Number 2
Mick Scully

I am not like the others. Is that correct? It is undeniable that I am like them in that I am a criminal: I lie; I steal; I kill. So, what do I mean when I say I am not like them? Two things. First, for me this is a life choice. A vocation, even. A craft, certainly. That is how I think of it. Which brings me to the second difference. I am educated. I have been to university. I read – wait for it – philosophy. It is true I dropped out in the second year. But that was a choice I made. I was not thrown out. My tutors considered me an excellent student. But I had recognized my calling.

Choice interests me. It is not as plentiful in our lives as people imagine. I chose to leave university. I chose this life. I choose to perform the morally reprehensible. Have you read Jean Genet? Not even in translation? You should. There are no secrets there. I wish I had met that man. I am straight but I think I would have let him fuck me. No. I hate that sort of attitude: indecisive; woolly thinking. I would have let him fuck me. Cross another barrier. What is life for, if not the experience of crashing through barriers? You should read William James on consciousness. I would recommend *Essays in Radical Empiricism* as a starting point. I think you will find it very enriching. There is a copy in Birmingham Central Library.

*

Do you see now that I am different? Different, and a little chameleon-like. Let me explain. If you take a bar like the Little Moscow – no, come with me. Let me take you there. The Little Moscow has always been a villains' place, a basement bar on the old Tyseley industrial estate; not that there's much industry there any more, only in the Little Moscow. It is late. Let's say it's a Friday. By eleven p.m. the bar will be full. Mostly men. This a space defined by the work of the men who inhabit it. Like a staff canteen. Or a university common room. Refreshment is enjoyed as men take ease from their labours. True, the actual work doesn't take place here, but it's what everyone talks about. There's no trade journal for the criminal fraternity, so bars like this have to fulfil that function. Networking. Planning. Paying off. Buying. Selling. At first glance just a bar but, upon closer observation, a hive of nefarious activity.

You will notice that most of the men are in groups. Some lounge against the pillars in pairs, or threes and fours. Larger groups congregate round the tables in the alcoves, or at those in this central area here. Some are playing snooker; as you can see there are two tables. There used to be a dartboard over there, on the wall by the third alcove, you see, where the plaster is chipped and broken. One night a barman was hit in the eye by a dart, and then in the other eye. He had upset somebody. So. It was double top for him. After that Fat Alex removed the board; health and safety.

There are a few other loners who come down here. Office, before he was banged up. Joey Hayes, after his brother Danny got maimed. The occasional guy from another territory, after work or information, or looking to recruit away from patch.

There's something about this place, don't you think? Genet would have recognized it. Look at those guys at the snooker table: the way they move around one another; the way they hold their cues. There's an unspoken respect for personal space in here; prison training. Body tension; everyone is on their guard. Look at those two standing by the fruit machine, they're motionless, but look at the eyes. See the way they dart around? They know everything that's going on. The tension is a language here. When you learn it you know who is up to what.

Right. Now you have the flavour of the place, look at me. See the difference? It's not just the suit, the tie, the polished shoes, though I certainly stand out from the puffa jacket and trainers crew. The wine? Yes, that makes a difference. It's how I got my name, Vino. I'm the only man in here who drinks wine. And the briefcase. Certainly. But look at my posture; the body language. No leaning against the wall – that indicates psychological insecurity, a need to disappear, fade into the background, become part of the place. There's nothing inconspicuous about me. I stand here, occupying the space all around me. My independence shines like a spotlight in this gloomy hole. I stand here, upright, relaxed – and no one messes.

I've had to prove myself, of course. Who d'you think threw the fucking darts? And I've used the canal outside. Nifty with a screwdriver, too. So. No one messes. It's their choice. And it's the right one.

Here's something for you. If I told you four of the men in here right now are killers, could you pick them out? I'd give good odds you couldn't. What about Darren, over there? The kid in the leather jacket, playing snooker. Such a baby face. Oozes innocence. Those baby-blue eyes. Like a girl's. Or old George, talking to the gut with the turban. Or what about the turban? Looks like he can handle himself. Maybe he's one. Or me? Do I look like a killer? More like a lawyer, or an advertising executive, surely. Genet would have picked us out. Stood on the steps, scanned the bar, sniffed a little, then lifted his finger and pointed. That one's a killer. That one's a thief. That one would like to be a killer, but he hasn't got it in him, what these men would call bottle.

You can tell I'm fit, can't you? Just by looking at me. The way I stand. And walk. I don't swagger. Just stroll around with casual, easy confidence. It marks me out. It's the gym work. I go to the Barton, a boxing gym above the Dove. I love the gym. Barriers again, you see. Pushing through the pain. You've got to. Keep pushing. Keep crashing through. Prove you're alive.

I'm proud of my body. If you were to see me naked. Genet would have loved me. I was with a woman last week. I'd stripped her off, and she was lying on the bed. I unbuttoned my shirt and the breath just whistled out of her. Most women tell me I've got a good body, but this was better: her eyes glued to my chest and the breath whistling out of her. When I dropped my pants she just went, 'Jesus Christ'; drove me crazy that did. I nearly shot there and then.

I used to tell myself I'd never kill a child. But. I am a killer. It's the job. A function. You are or you're not. You can't get picky over details.

'It's a warning, Vino,' Mr Rodrigo said to me. 'The only way we can deal with this bloke. It's got to be done.'

You're wondering how all this started, aren't you? Why a philosophy student chooses to abandon his studies and become a criminal. As with any vocation, it's there in the background, from childhood probably, nagging away. At school I was one of the good boys, kept my head down, studied hard. It was very important to my parents that I did well, I knew that. But while I was busy learning, I kept wondering – what would it be like? To smash a window? Steal the school fund? Put ground glass in someone's dinner?

*

Then one day in my second year at university. I'd been rereading *Crime and Punishment*. Dostoyevsky. I decided. I chose. Yes. I will become a criminal. So. I came into the city, not quite certain what I was going to do. I thought I would start with shoplifting. It seemed logical. A taster.

I went into Rackhams. I thought I would just get a couple of shirts, a tie or two. But. Travelling upward on the escalator, my attention was taken by a middle-aged woman on the step above me. She was nothing like the money-lender Raskolnikov kills, but she brought her to my mind. A nondescript woman really, two loaded shopping bags propped against her short legs. Very tidy. Very neat. Spectacles. Blonde hair. Smelling of unobtrusive perfume. Nothing you could be allergic to. Sensibly dressed. Respectable. Harmless.

I followed her. Watched her closely as she meandered among racks of clothes. Flicking through them. Lifting price tags. Removing a hanger. Holding the dangling garment in front of her to get an idea of size, then shuffling off to check its suitability in a mirror. While she was in a changing room I took three tops and a skirt from the racks she'd been surveying so assiduously. I folded them up, neat and small. When she returned from the changing room, leaving her bags on the floor beside the racks to drag yet another garment to the mirror, I popped my haul into one of her bags, pushing it down beneath the shopping. Then the tension. Delightful in its way. My first taste of it. Like your first hit of a drug, or your first beer. *I'm not sure I like this. Shall I stop now?* But the feeling is enticing, everything suddenly vibrant; enlarged, it seems.

She dithered around for quite a while. Was very tempted by a lavender top. She kept lifting the price tag and staring at it, as if hoping the amount printed there would magically reduce. A very indecisive woman. In the end she decided against. Shrugging her shoulders, she returned the hanger to the rail for the final time, paused as if saying goodbye to it, then marched bravely away, creating a tiny breeze which caused the fringe of tags beneath the clothes to sway sadly. Without looking back she took the escalator and made for the door.

Her face was exquisite when the alarm sounded and two women store detectives hastily surrounded her, one grabbing her arm. They led her quickly back into the store and went through her bags, right there in front of everyone. When they pulled the blouses out, her face crumpled. Confusion sweating out of it. She had to take her glasses off. I could see a leg shaking.

It was as they were insisting the frightened woman accompany them to an office, and she was vainly trying to articulate that some terrible mistake had occurred, that I approached the trio. It was to one of the detectives that I spoke, affecting a slight breathlessness. 'Excuse me. I've been looking for someone to report to. I saw this lady put some clothes in her bag. A couple of minutes ago.'

Her face elongated. The mouth falling open to form an oval. Glazed eyes grasping for some reality. Even when she gave her name and address she sounded doubtful.

But she'd got it right. I went there. Just watching. It was good training for me. Keeping an eye on the subject. Making myself invisible. Watching her come and go. Watching the family come and go.

As the day she was due in court approached she stopped going out. She just sat in a chair. Not watching television. Not reading. Sometimes she had the radio on, Radio 2, but not often. Mostly she just sat in silence. Depressed, I suppose.

In the afternoon of the day before her case I called round. She took a little time to answer the bell. Recognized me immediately. That jelly face. It was all over the place. Crumpled eyes. The mouth forming an oval again. Quivering chin.

'I hope I'm not disturbing you. I've called because I'm so worried. I think I might have made a terrible mistake.' That had her. She invited me in immediately. Sat me down in the silent lounge. Went into the kitchen to make tea.

There was almost relief when she realized what I was really there for. There often is with subjects. I crept down the stairs with a sheet. She hadn't heard me. Was just opening the fridge, and there I was. A sympathetic, reassuring smile on my face. Don't worry, it said, soon be over. Leave it all to me. Ever since, that smile has always returned at this point in my work, like a reflex. I call it Secret Smile Number 2.

It was all very simple and straightforward. Not much of a struggle. A squawk or two as I coiled the sheet around her neck. Shaking like a leaf as I led her up the stairs. Her glasses fell off and bounced across the carpet. Her eyes looked like they had in Rackhams. There was a little muted sound as I attached the sheet to the banister; sobbing, I think. Then a decisive shove. That was the noisiest bit: the banister creaking a protest; some hawking and hacking as she squirmed about. But it was soon over. And then she shat herself.

The only coverage it got was in the *Evening Mail*. DOCTOR'S SECRETARY COMMITS SUICIDE PRIOR TO SHOPLIFTING CASE. Not the snappiest headline in the world, is it? I've had better since. I went to the inquest. Heard all about her depression, shame, her total inability to accept what she had done, terror of the court hearing. No one was surprised she couldn't face it. Her husband said he blamed himself for not staying at home with her that week.

That was my first press cutting. I still have it. I've kept them all. And there have been some pretty big ones since, I can assure you. I'm talking national and international press here, not poxy local rags.

So. The decision had been made and acted upon. I considered whether the Rackhams case, as I refer to it in my files, was just a one-off – a young man's natural desire for experience. Curiosity. But no. It was more than this. There was a danger, however, one I recognized immediately, that I might become just a casual killer, stalking and taking opportunities where they occurred. I didn't want that. I wanted to be more useful. I wanted a career.

That was when I went to the Little Moscow for the first time. Just to discover what was available. Get a few names. Contacts. There I learned about Andy Crawford, known at one time as Black Andy, although no one dares to call him that to his face any more. He started off working for the Sanchez brothers at the Cascade when they were the big noise in the city, taking the place over when Ramon retired. Now Andy's based at the Barcelona Club, a very tasty outfit, casino and nightclub. He still owns the Cascade, plus several other clubs, bars and saunas. If this was the world I had chosen, I wanted to be with the top people.

I wasn't surprised Crawford was wary when I eventually managed to see him in the Barcelona. People like him have to be careful. And I had no real CV at the time. I could have been any lunatic, except I was smart, articulate, confident. He was intrigued. As I expected. I told him about the Rackhams case, showed him my press cutting. He was taken aback. But. I had decided what I needed to do. 'I would like to come back in a day or two, if I may. Discuss this matter further. Then I will show you more evidence of what I can do. In the meantime, bear St Martin's in mind.' That was the first time I used Secret Smile Number 1. Not meant for subjects – that's Number 2 and is very different – but for clients. It beams confidence, but has something of a mysterious quality to it. A touch sinister perhaps. I've never practised either smile. They just came to me. That's when you can be certain that you're a natural at something, when you discover you have all the little flourishes already programmed in. That was

Raskolnikov's problem, in my opinion. He wasn't a natural. His killing *was* obscene because it was obscene to *him*. I'm not like that.

It was an easy option. I knew that. The old tramp was well known around the fringes of the city. Used to push a battered supermarket trolley filled with old rags and bottles around. He was always in the market and the Bull Ring towards the end of the day. Traders gave him left-overs. I believe some of the restaurants helped him out. There were three or four places he slept, but at this time of year the steps of St Martin's Church was his favourite, tucked in close to the big wooden doors.

This one was easy. It wasn't until much later, when my career really took off, that I had to start using my brain. A rope seemed the obvious tool. But then I wanted to show Crawford that I could be ruthless. A knife or an axe through the throat might impress. Or a beheading. It would be more challenging too. I'd never used a knife at that time. But I tried to see things from Crawford's point of view. Those forms were showy. Messy. They carried the potential for too many hazards. He might think he had a lunatic on his hands. If efficiency were to be my selling point, then I should go for the cleanest, simplest method.

He knew all about it when I went to see him a week later; the *Evening Mail* had used the story on the front page. Crawford's attitude towards me was quite different this time. I was offered payroll there and then. But that wasn't what I wanted. I knew right from the start that the way to the top in this work is to remain freelance. Not be part of any organization. Consider a job offered, do it if you want to, collect and out. That's the way I've always played it.

I can laugh about it now, but at the time I was insulted, truly. Nearly turned it down. It was a dog. To put the frighteners on a guy. His mother's guide dog. It wasn't what

I was expecting for my first commission, but I put as much effort into its planning and execution as I have into all my subsequent work. It was sorted within a couple of days, and I received my first pay. That was the day I went to see my tutor, Dr Catherine Harrad, and told her I was leaving the course. She was very disappointed. Tried to talk me out of it. But eventually conceded that it was my choice.

Let me show you a trick. Look at this. My palm. OK? Steady as a rock, right? Now the lighter. Keep your eyes on my palm. See the flame lick at it. But still steady as a rock, right? I've been able to do this since I was a boy. Now watch this. I'm going to hold the flame still. Here. Just beneath the thumb. Right. One. Two. Three. Four. Five. Six. Seven. Eight. Nine. Ten. Impressed? I've gone longer. Fifteen. Sixteen. You get the point. That will blister now in a couple of minutes.

Pain interests me. I've considered whether I'm a sadist, but I'm not. When I sleep with a woman I have no desire to hurt her. Just the opposite. I've received many compliments on my tenderness and attentiveness. I often spend time before a conquest planning how I can give maximum pleasure and satisfaction.

I enjoy a good sex life. But you'd expect that, looking at me, wouldn't you? I haven't found love yet, but it's my choice. A decision I've made. But I get plenty of sex. Women love my body. I do very well with librarians.

Do you know the *Leningrad Symphony* by Shostakovich? Now that's music. Stirs the spirit. It gets me marching. All precision and control. Determination and power. I play it repeatedly before I go out on an important job, then again in the car on the way. It is still in my mind as I work, like the soundtrack of a film I'm starring in. It helps me work efficiently.

Don't get the impression that the work I do is easy. Popular culture presents it that way, but it's not. Certain elements still have the power to shock and make me consider. Children are difficult. Originally they were a no-go area, but I came to see this was just another barrier – one I had to crash through if I was to develop. We limit our human potential if we allow ourselves to accept barriers. I have chosen this way of life. There is no point in being squeamish. Elimination is elimination. They're there. And then they're not. Any other attitude is hypocritical. Indulgent.

'This is the way it's got to be, I'm afraid, Vino,' Mr Rodrigo said, tutting as he leaned back in his big, leather chair. 'It's a warning. This man is too important to eliminate at this stage. But he's being obstructive. Very, very obstructive. Costing me and my associates a fortune because of his stubborn greed. He's ignored the shots we've fired across his bows, and now he thinks he has us beaten. But he hasn't. So now we have to apply very severe pressure indeed.'

He's got extremely fat hands, Mr Rodrigo. The fat bulges around his gold rings. You'd have to cut off his fingers to remove them. I've never seen him without a cigar.

'To be frank, Vino, the cunt's got far too big for his boots. I'm sorry to say. The only way to deal with someone like him is to come down hard. It has to be his kiddie.'

'How old?'

'Eight.' He skimmed an envelope across the surface of his wide wooden desk. Inside were three photographs of the child. One in school uniform. There was also an information sheet. Address of his school. Judo class he attends on Saturday mornings. Times he leaves the house. Returns. Routes. Names, addresses and telephone numbers of friends. Even the football team he supports – Manchester United. Why don't kids support their local team any more? Now they only want to support the most successful teams. It's all part of the disintegration of community spirit.

Mr Rodrigo stretched back and rubbed his belly; his chair squeaked. 'You're the only one I'd trust with a job as crucial as this, Vino.' He leaned forward and his belly wedged itself close against the edge of the desk. With his head stretching over it towards me he looked like a turtle. He exhaled cigar smoke. 'You're a consummate professional, Vino. The best in this city, without a doubt – the country, possibly. You're in demand internationally now, aren't you? I know that. I want the best, Vino. And you know I'm willing to pay for it.'

Now, I'm not a fool. I'm not susceptible to flattery. That's for the weak-minded. Of course, that's what Mr Rodrigo was trying to do. Seduce my services from me through flattery. But, while I haven't checked the definition of the word in a dictionary recently, my understanding is that just because the intention behind making a statement is to flatter, it doesn't mean that statement is false. What Mr Rodrigo said was true.

The job was going to be done. He's a very determined man. What Mr Rodrigo wants to happen usually happens. So. If it wasn't me, it'd be someone else. And at least I'd do it efficiently.

I was telling you about the subject. It was a disturbing proposal, a child, I have to be honest. But I had a choice, and I made it. I accepted the commission. But let me show you that it is more complex than these words might suggest. Come with me. To the school he attended. St Alphage in Edgbaston. A very good prep school. Private, of course. There he is. I recognize him immediately from the photographs. That one there. With the floppy hair. Galloping around with the ginger-haired lad. Children have so much energy, don't they? A real live wire.

I have to put a lot of background work into my commissions. I hate using clichés, but that ugly aphorism – the six Ps, Perfect Preparation Prevents Piss Poor Performance –

is true. Everything is in the preparation. Like this, outside
the school playground. Checking the times I've been given.
It would be absurd to take them as read. The time he leaves
the house. The time he returns. All this has to be checked.
Who picks him up? Is it always the same person? Do they
arrive on time? Or is he ever kept waiting? Is it always the
same vehicle? The same route? The house has to be cased
too. Where's his bedroom? The kitchen? Where does he
watch television? Does he play out in the garden after
school? Or is he one of those youngsters who sits in front
of a computer for hours? All the time I am considering –
can I take him alone or does someone else have to come
with him? His mother? The mother of a pal who collects
him from school and drops him off at home? A teacher
perhaps? Or the chap who runs the judo class? Not that it
matters, as long as it's not the father, that's in the contract.
He's got to suffer in another way.

I did the job this morning. There was a small hitch. I had
decided to take him out in the playground, from the cover
of the overgrown laurel bushes beside the school railing.
Playtime starts at eleven o'clock. At ten to, it started to
rain. Quite heavily. Well, they're not going to send kids out
in rain, are they? Not these days. It was different when I
was that age. Go out and get some fresh air, they would
say, even if it was chucking it down, but fortunately we've
moved on since then.

I hear the bell ringing for break. Some things don't
change. No electronic beeping or space-age announcement.
It sounds just as it did when I was at school. That shrill
jangling that bounces off the walls for six seconds,
impossible to ignore. It's still raining, but more lightly, just
a fine drizzle now. The sky is lightening a little, too. My
observations have shown that approximately ninety
seconds after the bell rings the first of the children emerge
from the building. The subject is usually among them.

Keen to escape the confinement of the classroom, he dashes around, before gradually making his way with his friend to this end of the playground, near the laurel bushes.

Three minutes and not a child in sight, although the rain is now very fine, hardly anything at all. Surely the teachers won't keep them cooped up inside for the entire twenty minutes? It isn't healthy. It sounds like they're all running wild in there. The windows are steaming up. Usually, when the children are inside, all that is heard are the organized sounds of a school at work: teachers' voices; children singing along to a clunky performance on an out-of-tune piano; the thump of balls from the small hall which doubles as a gymnasium.

Things don't look promising. Plan B might be the solution. Tonight. At home. He sits in front of the television with a bowl of cereal. Four forty-five is the time I've pencilled in. Then something marvellous happens. The rain stops. The sun leaps out. And here they come. They're letting them out. Of course, the pattern of arrival I have become so familiar with in the last few days is likely to be disrupted, but we will see.

I don't know what's been going on this morning but the children I recognize from the subject's class all have a label stuck to their chest like a target, their names printed in bright, crayon-coloured letters. *Sophie Eccles*; *Lucy Ross*; *Ian Merrick*. A straggly stream, rather than the abrupt tide that normally sweeps through the door. Perhaps they're not all coming out. Some may have been given the option of staying put. How things have changed. But based upon my observations of the subject I think he would choose to get out of the building, out into the freedom of the fresh air. And I'm right, for here he comes. Hurtling down the steps and making for a puddle which he stamps in, spraying water over a pair of girls who shriek their displeasure. He is delighted. Naughty boy. It makes me smile.

Now he is running this way. I can read his name, *David Kohler*, stuck to the front of his maroon jersey. A useful, if unnecessary, confirmation of identity. The speed at which this lad moves is something to which I have had to give serious consideration. The pattern is: he darts about wildly for a couple of minutes, then halts abruptly as if he's run out of steam. He dawdles around for a while, then, with his energy replenished, he's off again. A mischievous boy, he will often jump onto the back of another lad. I've seen a couple of mock fights this week that I thought were going to turn into the real thing. I bet he's a handful in the classroom. A rather tasty young teacher with a good line in tight sweaters, and the figure to do them justice, usually joins the children after seven or eight minutes, and stays for about ten, wandering around vaguely, coffee cup in hand. No sign of her yet.

The only way to deal with the problem of movement is to take aim when the subject is in a stationary position, then let the sights follow him like a video camera until he adopts another stationary position.

He's up this end now. Almost touching distance. Splashing about in a large puddle just inside the perimeter rails, ruining his expensive school shoes. He kicks water up at his ginger pal, turns and flees. He certainly can run. But the soaked boy is too busy laughing and rubbing water from his eyes to give chase. This is it. At a safe distance from his chum he stops and turns to see if he's being pursued. He is roaring with laughter at his dripping friend. I'm smiling too, though unfortunately he can't see it. Secret Smile Number 2. I squeeze on the trigger. One shot. The job is done.

Straight out of the bushes and away. Almost as soon as the shot is fired the clouds are back. Within a minute the rain has returned. The sunshine was just a lucky break. With this soft ground there'll be footprints. That's OK. My first job is always to burn the gear: trainers, two sizes too large; the cheap tracksuit. The gun goes in a plastic sports bag. That will burn too. To the casual passer-by I'm just some guy on the way to the gym. The ashes are carefully collected into a bag of bricks and slung into the canal. The garden incinerator hosed down with weed killer. The chemical reaction destroys all forensic. The gun goes safely back into storage. In no time, all is done and I'm phoning my report of accomplishment in to Mr Rodrigo. Then a little relaxation. Unwind. I like to listen to Bach's *Goldberg Variations* after a job. It's very tense work, highly concentrated, and this music is perfect for rehabilitating the spirit. I would recommend it.

I've worked all over, you know. But Birmingham is my favourite city. I'd put Belgrade second. Very under-rated. I sometimes toy with the idea of a second home there. But Birmingham will always be my real home. I'm at peace in this city. I know it so well. Know where everything is. Don't have to think about it. Like a poem learned by heart in primary school. You never lose it. They don't do that any more. Get children to learn poetry by rote. It's a pity in my opinion. Poetry can be a great source of comfort. And insight. That's why poems are so often read at funerals.

I'm enjoying our little chat. I hope you are. I don't often open up like this. Is it frustrating for you? Do you wish you could talk back? Well, now's your opportunity. In a minute I'm going to remove the gag. And when I do, I want the answer to a question. Are you going to persuade your husband to co-operate with Mr Rodrigo, once and for all? Yes or no? If the answer is yes, which I feel sure it will be, although of course the choice is yours, all this unpleasantness will be at an end. And you have another child to think of, I believe, Emily. And there's your own security. The police can be of no help, as I'm sure you know. There's no evidence, and your husband is far too entrenched in matters that, shall we say, are not strictly within the law for the police to be a realistic option. If everything came out he'd probably end up doing the longer sentence. And where would that leave you and Emily, Mrs Kohler? Revenge is a powerful concept in the world your husband has dipped his toe into. Think about the men of the Little Moscow. Just sitting. Hanging around. Waiting for something to come up. An offer.

Mr Rodrigo would like what happened to David this morning to be an end to the matter. And I'm sure you and Mr Kohler would too.

Just before I remove the gag, Mrs Kohler, let me play you this. On my Walkman. Beautiful, isn't it? It's the *Leningrad Symphony* by Shostakovich. You can see how it affects me. Can't you?

Look, Mrs Kohler. You see this. This is Secret Smile Number 2. You will be the first person to have seen it and be allowed to remember it. See. Of course, if you ever see it again – but best not go into that, eh? It's not necessary, is it? I'm sure everything is resolved.

Rain Damage
Mick Scully

Keeley is upstairs on the number eighteen. As it rounds the corner onto the estate the bags at her feet tilt against her leg. She likes the feeling, is reassured by it. Her shopping. She looks down. They are such lovely bags. Each states the name of the shop where the purchase was made. And these bags are substantial. With proper handles. Quality. They have a shape and will stand upright when empty. Inside are the clothes she's bought: beautiful, beautiful garments. Quality shops. Designer.

Beyond the bus the estate passes by, and Keeley looks out onto it. It is lovely in the spring sunshine that subdues the grey concrete frames of the tower blocks and glitters upon the layers of glass they contain. Keeley loves the gleaming glass oblongs reflecting the day's sunlight in a black glitter. They are so glamorous; like Las Vegas, she thinks.

Two stops to go. She is now the only passenger upstairs so she doesn't have to be discreet. Keeley takes the thin plastic supermarket bags from her coat pocket, and carefully transfers the new clothes from their original bags. She folds the empty bags neatly and pushes them down beside the clothes. She is nearly home. She dislikes this exercise, but accepts that it would be foolish to be seen carrying bags from expensive shops.

At the foot of Walton Towers is Mrs Nayer's General Store. It is a cage. The outside imprisoned in a mesh of wired panelling. There can be no window-shopping here. Mrs Nayer is behind the counter. Sabre, her Alsatian, gets up and moves cautiously towards Keeley, sniffing at her feet.

'Hello, Keeley. Isn't it lovely today? So sunny. You have been shopping.'

'Yes, Mrs Nayer.' The dog starts to sniff at her bags.

'Sabre! Sabre! Come here. Sabre!' The dog turns heel and saunters back to Mrs Nayer behind the counter. 'I haven't seen you for a few days. Have you been sick?'

'No, Mrs Nayer. Everything is fine.'

'I have your magazines,' the shopkeeper says, stooping beneath the counter, then rising with the three magazines Keeley buys every week. Mrs Nayer lays them one by one on the counter, as if she were dealing cards, or giving a Tarot reading. '*M Girl. Heatwave. OK.*'

Keeley takes the lift to the seventh floor. She lives in the middle of the building. There is no one on the landing as she takes her key from her pocket and enters her flat. What time is it? One fifteen. She has done well today. There is no problem about time; if he should call today she will be here.

She goes into the kitchen where she removes the garments from the cheap bags and – checking they're not in any way crumpled – restores them to their original bags, which she places in a row on the kitchen floor. She recalls a picture in one of her magazines of Victoria Beckham. Walking through the streets carrying lots of bags. Just like these. She looks at them. Her shopping. When Victoria arrives home her purchases will be placed in the hallway of her lovely house, in a row probably, just as these are. She will have people to put the clothes away for her. Lift them gently from their bags and hang them carefully.

She puts the magazines on the kitchen table. She will make an omelette for lunch. With a tomato salad. And she'll select one of the magazines to read as she eats. She's glad she didn't succumb to temptation and buy that cream doughnut to bring back for dessert. Keeley slides her hand across her belly. There is yoghurt in the fridge.

Keeley feels sorry for Geri Halliwell. She has been through a lot. Anorexia. A loss of confidence. And she's been unlucky in love. She stares down at the three pictures of the singer with her new boyfriend – a fitness instructor – that fill the page. He looks nice. Perhaps he will make her happy. Keeley hopes so.

When Jed comes she makes him coffee. He sees the bags, and smiles. She has always liked his smile. Even at first. It was different then, of course.

'Bin shoppin'?' he asks.

She shows him the clothes she's bought. He admires them; compliments her on her taste. 'You've got great taste, Keel. Like a model, you are.' He says he would like to see her in the black dress. Will she put it on for him? But when she has removed her jeans and top and is reaching for the dress he rises from the kitchen stool and, moving in behind her, encloses her in his arms. She isn't surprised. She is pleased, she likes Jed. Perhaps she shouldn't after what he did. But he has tried to make it up to her. They all have.

He is a kind lover. He wants to please her and is more gentle than you would expect from the look of him. She likes these visits; these hours with him in the bedroom. He is never in a hurry to get away. Sometimes when he visits they don't have sex, but mostly they do. It's just sort of happened like this. Fate, she supposes. There is a worry she has though. That one day the visits will clash. That he will turn up when the other one is here – or the other way round. But she corrects herself. She is being foolish. Before

Jed goes, he reaches into his leather jacket and gives her the brown envelope. 'From the Boss,' he says, and drops it onto the kitchen table. She never opens it while he is here. When he is gone she will put it safely away in her dressing-table drawer and tomorrow she will take the money to the post office.

She feels a little sad when Jed leaves. He's a nice bloke and she won't see him for a month. Maybe even longer. Sometimes the Boss sends someone else.

When he has gone she puts her new clothes on. Looks at herself in the mirror. Feels the beautiful clothes, imagines photographs, runs her hand gently over the fabrics, places them on the bed and admires their shapes, design. When she eventually puts them away in her wardrobe with the others, she remembers some pictures she saw of Jennifer Aniston's home – a room full of clothes, all arranged by colour. It was wonderful. Rows and rows of shoes. Like a shop.

Keeley sits in the kitchen listening to music on the radio. Kylie is singing about being lucky. It is getting dark now. She knows she is lucky to have such lovely clothes. But she can't enjoy this thought as she would like to. This happens sometimes. The sadness comes to her. She goes to the window and looks down on the lights of the estate. She must control these dark thoughts. She once read an interview with Cate Blanchett that said she tried to turn every negative into a positive – that's what she must do too.

There was £500 in the envelope when she counted it out the next day. She took it to the post office; the Stirchley branch. It wasn't sensible to use the local one where she collected her benefits.

Some months there was more than this. It all depended. On what, she wasn't sure. At first there'd been a thousand every month, but that only lasted for a while. It seemed to be levelling out at around five hundred now. She doesn't mind. She was careful. Every few weeks she went into town, to the Mailbox where the designer shops are, and treated herself. But apart from that she was careful.

Her lounge is beautiful. She paid for it out of the early money. Jed and another man decorated it for nothing; she supposed he felt he owed her. Guilt. She got her ideas from magazines and the furniture from Habitat. It is such a lovely room. She doesn't go into it very much – she wants to keep it nice, but sometimes she just stands outside the door looking in. It is like a photograph. Jed decorated the other rooms for her too; the whole flat was lovely, she was lucky – but the lounge was the best.

Craig Carrow parked his GTI at the foot of Walton Towers, and reached across for the bunch of tulips from the back seat. He alarmed the car and looked round; everything seemed all right. Inside, a few kids hanging around the lobby, smoking and shouting at each other, stared at him, but he recognized none of them.

He used the stairs. He hated these tower blocks. Peeling, stinking, graffitied pits in which the cold concrete steps seemed to go on for ever. There was always further to climb. More kids were messing around somewhere further up. Their shouts echoed down the hollow of the stairwell and his footsteps echoed up to them.

'Nigga!' The shouted word, followed by shrieks of laughter, slithered down the long water stains that marked the naked brick walls. A gob of spit flew down and spattered on the rail, just missing his hand. More verbal graffiti followed it.

He should turn round; get out of this god-forsaken place. He knew now why he hadn't been for a while. He might be climbing upwards, but in reality this was a descent. Still, he was horny; had been thinking about her for most of the week, longer probably. He liked her, felt sorry for her after what had happened. Also, he knew she still got visits from Jed Owen, though why she let that scum anywhere near her after what he did, he couldn't imagine. Or rather he could. Soon after, the place was done up. Pretty expensive too, tasteful; like her clothes.

He'd tried at the beginning to get her to talk. She could have been the key to everything. At the time he'd accepted that she was shocked, confused; couldn't talk about it. 'Give her time,' his old governor, Riley, had told him. So he had. Just hung on in there. And there were the perks. But eventually he knew she'd been got at. No other explanation.

Another gob of spit sailed past. More whoops of laughter drifted into the space below. He turned off towards her flat through the battered fire door marked 7.

She'd obviously seen him through the spy-hole, but she still seemed surprised when she opened the door. She looked down and saw the flowers. He enjoyed her delight. There was no doubt about it, she was a very attractive girl. She knew how to make the best of herself.

'I can go if it's not convenient,' he whispered, smiling and raising the red tulips.

'No. It's fine. A nice surprise. Come in.'

They both knew why he was there and though they went through the motions – a cup of coffee, she cooing about the tulips, arranging them in a vase and taking it into the lounge, complimenting him on his appearance, 'A beautiful suit, Craig. You must be doing all right' – it wasn't long before they were in bed, athletically screwing. Christ! This was what he needed. He was going to get it all out of his system tonight; fuck himself sore.

He hadn't had a girlfriend for ages, and as they lay together during one of their pauses, she with her head on his chest, he playing his fingers through her hair, he thought, I must come and see her more often, like before. She's nice.

'You OK?' he asked.

'Lovely,' she sighed, and smoothed her tongue across his nipple, like a kid with ice cream.

There had been a time when he visited regularly. Sometimes when he was on duty; sometimes in the middle of the night. If everything was quiet he might just pop round. She always welcomed him, dozy with sleep, but happy to see him, give him an hour or so. She said he had been good to her when she needed it.

Then it had all gone wrong. One night he came round in the patrol car. Left it outside, and it was nicked. So much trouble that had caused him. Demotion. He ended up on Traffic. For a while he was so disappointed, so angry with himself, he couldn't come round. But that was the past. No squad cars any more. Professionally things were going well. It was just his sex life that was crap. Or had been. Keeley's tongue was moving down his chest, into his belly button where it pushed a gasp out of him before moving on.

'It's past eleven. I must go.' He pushed back the duvet.

'You can stay the night if you want.'

'I'd love to. But shift work. You know.'

She said nothing more. That was one of the good things about her, she never made anything difficult. No pressure. Cool.

'I'll pop in again soon,' he said, zipping his fly. 'If that's OK?'

'You're always welcome,' she said. 'It's always nice to see you.'

Keeley couldn't get back to sleep after Craig left. She'd been dozing in his arms when he realized the time, but now she was wide awake. To see him out she'd put on a beautiful silk kimono-style dressing gown. She loved the feel of the fabric against her skin. She'd noticed herself in the bedroom mirror as she'd gone with him to the door. It was so glamorous. From the kitchen window she watched the rear lights of his car winding away from the estate. She was glad his car was OK. It was always a risk round here. And there had been such trouble when the police car had been stolen. She'd thought he wouldn't come again. She was glad he'd visited tonight though. They'd both been this week, which was nice, and she had the feeling Craig would come back soon too.

Jed Owen has a bad feeling about this job. Nothing he can put his finger on. Just a feeling. Then, as if in confirmation, rain. It's been the sunniest spring for years, everyone walking around in shades, like California, and girls in short summer dresses. Then, today. Grey as communism all morning. As soon as he stole the Volvo it started pissing down, and it hasn't stopped. Rain to put the shite up Noah. Working in weather like this always makes Jed uneasy; an extra hazard, one he could do without.

He picks the other two up. Coy and Johnny Day. Drowned rats huddling in the doorway waiting for him. 'Got the fucking scuba gear?' Coy asks humourlessly as he gets into the seat beside Jed. Johnny gets in the back. He's carrying a sports bag with the gear: masks, gemmy-coshes, etc.

Then over to Handsworth. Priory Road. Slow cruise down the street and there it is, exactly where it's supposed to be. A black Honda Civic. Nothing too flashy. Two fifteen. Plenty of time. Info says they'll leave between two thirty and three. On the mobi to Darryl. 'Everything running to order. Except for the bastard rain. You?' He tells Jed he's picked up a Toyota, gives him the reg. 'OK. See you there.' He turns to the other two men. 'He's ready and waiting. Blue Toyota. W874 KLG.' Jed turns the engine, the wipers spring into action. He waits for a gap in the traffic, pulls out and heads for Wharburton Hill.

No one says much. There's reggae coming from the radio but they can still hear the angry thump of rain against the car roof. The plan is simple, but then they usually are – the plans. Doberman Crew are making a big shift – money for the London laundry and stock for the London outlets, a fair bit of it: H, coke, a lot of Es apparently, a fair wad of crack, plus sundries. Doberman are a Brum outfit. But expanding bloody fast. Tails in Manchester and Liverpool. Now a London partnership. Suppliers only – for now. In return for healthy prices they get their cleaning done – but with their ambition, who knows?

They're moving it all nice and quiet, the info says. Two-man job. Legit motor. Belongs to Strombo. Cheeky git, using his own motor. Nice afternoon run down the Smoke. All nice and easy. That's what Strombo thinks. Wait till he hits Wharburton Hill. That's where they get company.

'I still don't understand why we didn't just storm Priory Road. Take it off them there. Just before they left,' Johnny Day says from the back of the car, as if he's been pondering this question for some time.

Coy sighs. 'Because there are more fuckin' guns in that place than Baghdad. That's why.'

Johnny considers this and seems to accept the point. Under his leather jacket he's wearing the Villa shirt he always wears for jobs. He's a Baggies man, the whole family is, but thinks the shirt is some sort of decoy.

Darryl is there. In place. Jed pulls up ahead of him, onto the brow of the hill. Thank Christ the rain is easing off a bit. Johnny is unloading the sports bag. Masks. Coshes. He passes them forward, then gives the binoculars to Coy, who starts to scan the traffic at the foot of the hill for the Civic.

Waiting is always the worst. Jed's turned the radio off. Music does your head in at this stage. They all feel the tension. But at least the rain's stopped now. Coy never moves. Binoculars glued to the road, his breath wheezing in and out. But he's pretty cool really, just smokes too many fucking fags. Johnny Day sitting upright in the back, like a Samurai. Concentrating. Eyes closed. Waiting. And Jed, drumming his fingers on the steering wheel, then stopping because the last thing you want to do right now is irritate anybody. No point worrying. They'll come when they come.

At last. A single word from Coy – *OK* – and the handbrake is off, feet hit the pedals and Jed takes it away. He checks the mirror. Darryl pulling out behind him. Sweet. Halfway down the hill he spots the car. Estimate – distance, speed. Compute. All done in an instant. No problem. He's good at this, Jed. That's why he's here.

'Deep breaths, boys!' he yells as he accelerates hard towards the Civic. A chorus. All three men bawling their lungs out on impact: 'Yees!' Jed is good at this. As they lurch forward Jed can see it's a perfect hit. Rear door passenger side. Crumpled to fuck. The Civic wobbles, sways, swings, but doesn't tumble. Bumper cars from childhood visits to the fair flicker, for a second, through his mind, as he swings with the impact. He loved the fair when he was a kid – the lights, music, crowds. He thinks of candyfloss and goldfish in plastic bags.

Before the echo of ripping metal dies away the three men are out of the Volvo, racing round the Honda. Jed has his shooter out. Coy takes the driver. Gun in his ear. Johnny Day the car boot. A precise whack with the cosh and it flips open. Through the dark peepholes of his mask Jed stares into Strombo's wild, outraged eyes. His lips are moving but

Jed hears nothing but his own heart pounding, the gasps of his breath. There is a case on Strombo's lap. Jed jerks it away. Strombo's arm shoots up. The case is cuffed. Fuck it! About eight inches of chain attach the case to Strombo's wrist.

''E's cuffed the fuckin' thing,' Jed yells to Johnny Day, who's lifting boxes out of the boot, handing them across to Darryl.

'OK,' Johnny says, and he darts round the Volvo, leans into his bag, emerges with an axe. Darryl continues loading the boxes into the Toyota. Jed has Strombo out of the car, lying in the road. When Strombo sees Johnny Day approaching with the axe he recoils, tries to squirm away. Swearing his stinking head off. But Jed has him secure: knee in the chest; gun in the face. Strombo's driver, a wiry black guy with a shaved head and purple shades, sits quiet, facing straight ahead, aware only of Coy's gun rammed into his ear. Coy has his hand on top of the man's head, like he's holding him under water.

'Shall we take the fuckin' 'and as well?' Johnny Day says. Jed grabs the case, stretching the chain, and Strombo turns his head. Johnny Day brings the axe down neatly in the centre of the chain. Another tap and it divides.

'Guns!' Coy barks. The two men hand over their shooters. 'Phones!' Coy grinds the mobiles into the ground with his boot. Jed smacks the axe into the windscreen, frosting it. Puts a bullet into the nearside front tyre.

Then they're all in beside Darryl, Jed holding the case on his lap just as Strombo had. They cheer as Darryl turns the motor into life and wheels round in the road. 'Fuckin' ace work,' Darryl says.

Carrow peered through the front passenger window up into the leaden, incontinent sky. His head turned front, to the wide windscreen, weeping smears of colour, rumours of shape struggling to find form beyond the sluicing wipers. He couldn't see a fucking thing.

'You'll need to step on it, PP,' he muttered tersely to his partner, Paul Parker. 'We need to have them back in sight before the motorway.'

Parker winced and shrugged. There was no point in arguing with Carrow. He squeezed his foot onto the accelerator and started to overtake. In the back two other officers were attempting to play cards on a newspaper laid across their knees. They looked at each other; one strained forward to read the speedometer. The horn of a furious motorist blared at them aggressively.

'Fuck off,' Carrow responded, turning his head as if he could address the angry driver personally. 'We're fuckin' cops,' he sneered. The car swerved, suddenly and violently, tilting all four men to the left. Playing cards sailed away from the newspaper to the floor, some caught in the glove compartment. Another horn sounded. One of the officers in the back whistled, a brief call of shock, but no one said anything.

Carrow enjoyed this fact. He was the boss. It was a satisfying feeling. No one argued. He inserted a CD in the player, and Eddie Grant began to sing. Sunshine music to relax him. Groans from the back. 'Fuck off, you two. This is good music.' Guffaws from the back. Parker merely grinned.

Carrow wondered what these men thought of him. Not that it mattered. No, that wasn't true; of course it wasn't fucking true. Here he was: a governor now. DS Craig Carrow. He'd fucked up a little along the way, but now he was moving. Up. Up. Up. It was important his officers respected him. To be a good governor was what counted in the force. Reputation was all.

'Shit, Guv!' Carrow felt himself pushed forward, his seatbelt biting into his shoulder, then his chest as the impact continued. He heard a cry from the back.

'Look out,' Parker yelled, braking hard before Carrow had time to focus. Then he saw it. A smashed car, doors swinging open. A man lying in the gutter.

His mind worked quickly. Decision: it was more important now to get the pirates. Anger rose in him. He should have told Parker to put his foot down earlier, he'd been complacent. If they'd been closer they might have pulled in two teams; what a feather that would have been. But it was still possible. He hit Stop to kill Eddie Grant, pulled the radio mike, yelling 'Follow them! The pirates!' at Parker. 'And don't let them out of your fucking sight.'

Parker responded instantly, and the men inside the car tilted and swayed as the unmarked police car swerved into Wharburton Hill. 'Siren, sir?' Parker asked.

'Not yet. Let's give it a minute.' He started talking into the radio, instructing support to deal with the chaos at the foot of Wharburton Hill and explaining the change in their operational plan. As he spoke a thought glowed in his mind: *Yeah. It can still be done. Pull in the pirates together with Strombo's mob. That really would be cream in the coffee.*

Darryl's eyebrows narrowed in concentration. His eyes flickered between the road ahead and the road reflected in his rear-view mirror. He was uneasy about a Rover behind and had now reduced his speed. Could it be? Well, there was only one way to find out. He inhaled deeply and, pushing his foot hard down onto the accelerator, pulled out and aimed his vehicle into the narrow gap separating the two opposing trails of traffic. He knew someone further up would bottle out and let him in. Someone always did. You just had to keep your nerve and go for it. Most people couldn't. Aggression in driving, as with everything else in life, got you where you wanted to be.

His instinct was right. Before his passengers had a chance to protest at the sudden manoeuvre, through the wing mirror he saw the Rover pull away to follow him. Within seconds the siren started; traffic began to give way. The men in the Toyota with him swore as they swung with the speed of the car. He tuned them out. Concentration now. It was a bastard, this happening, but the wailing siren, like a syringeful of H, made an instant hit sending adrenalin burning through him, like sunlight, giving him the energy to enjoy the chase. Like a card shark, he had to deceive the eye with speed. Be fast; be sharp. And he was both these things. His clenched teeth jammed against each other, echoing the pressure his foot applied to the accelerator. In the interior mirror he watched the stricken face of a grey-haired man behind, caught between the mercilessly impatient sirening car and theirs, and not knowing what the fuck to do about it. Behind his spectacles his enlarged eyes danced in frightened confusion.

Darryl smiled to himself; mouthed silent thanks to the poor fucker behind. This should be OK. The others were saying nothing but their audible breathing held its own tense eloquence. It was all down to him. He wouldn't fail. Darryl smacked his foot into the brake. Everyone lurched forward. Yells of *What the fuck, Daz?* and *What ya doin', man?* tumbled around the car, but Darryl's foot was straight off the brake and ramming home the accelerator. His eyes stayed fast in the mirror. The smile returned. It had worked. The sudden red glow of brake lights had added to Greyhair's terror and he'd jammed his own brakes on. Darryl saw the pale, lined face swing forward, close to the windscreen, then, held by his seat belt, shudder and fall back, glasses sliding away from his nose. He stalled, of course, and the siren car, far too close, shunted into him. This was his moment.

'Hold onto your arses,' he yelled, as he spun into an arching right, straight into a side street. Beautiful! A cheer from the boys as they stabilized. Then the bad card. The joker; the ace of spades – call it what you like. A guy walks from between two parked vans, straight through their windscreen. Most of him in Darryl's lap. The car skitters and careers, dances giddily along the road, rubbing and nudging other cars, before burying its shame in the side of a bus. The impact sends the pedestrian flying back out through the mouth of the shattered windscreen, leaving a pool of blood in Darryl's crotch.

Jed should have been dazed. His neck was hurting, and the images that invaded his brain when the man stepped into their path were still burning away; but something, his thief's cunning perhaps, or the criminal instinct for survival, forced action from him. He punched at the passenger door beside him. Nothing. Then, finding courage he drove his hurting shoulder at it. Tearing, grinding metal. A soundtrack for the pain searing his neck. Another heave, and the door ground open providing just enough space for him to squeeze through, dragging the case behind him.

A shot was fired. *Poor baby*, a voice was saying. *Poor baby*. Rain dripped from his face like cold tears. There was shouting far away. Then Coy, lugging words like bricks into his ear: 'Run, you fuckin' fool. Run!'

'Go! Go! Go!' Other voices were yelling too; missiles coming at him. *Poor baby*, he told himself. 'Go!' Coy bawled. Then the noise that had held him enveloped found a space in his ears and shot straight through to his feet, so that he wobbled, or was he ducking missiles?

In front of him Johnny Day wobbled too, then keeled and fell bleeding at his feet. The other images, though: they were still a burning wreckage in his brain, smearing across what he was now seeing with his eyes. Another shot, and he turned. His feet started to move. Fast. Then faster. Another shot and faster still. The whole world was running behind him. He could hear their footsteps, splashing through the rain. The streets were shaking. Like an earthquake, like a volcano, like a war. Straight lines melted into contours, and he rounded them. They were still following him. He knew it though he couldn't hear them because of his own breath, whistling, hot piston jets forcing air in and out of his chest, pressing his legs over arcs of space, pushing his feet to hammer and pound. I am a machine. A tank. Unstoppable. He ran and ran, soaked with rain and sweat, holding the case close to his wounded chest.

When he saw a launderette it was like a brake, slowing him down. The Mermaid Launderette. Empty. He staggered in, like the end of a race. The finishing point. But he knew nothing was finished yet. Or perhaps now *everything* was.

Stupid prat you are, he mutters to himself as he strides round the shop, opening the door of each washing machine, peering in. Paranoid prat. He returns to the machine at the back. Throws the case in. Slams the door. Everything is shaking. He sits down, leans forward, panting, arms on his knees as if he's watching the racing on telly. He looks into the dark porthole; thinks of a diver's helmet. I've got some thinking time, he thinks.

He thinks he hears sirens, far away, but isn't sure. Lets the breaths ease down. Wipes the sweat, rain and tears from his face. The gun in his pocket is pushing against his balls like an erection. He leans back and takes it out. Puts it inside his jacket, close to his slowing heart. In the darkness of the porthole the pictures return. How can it happen twice? Am I cursed or something? I must be. Fucking cursed. He tries to rinse the images away, bleach them from his mind, but the video keeps going. Stupidly he wants some music. Loud, fast music. A soundtrack to wipe out reality. Only that can protect him. But there is no music. Even his breathing has quietened now. He has to take it. Face it. Look into the porthole behind which the case of money squats.

Two years ago. A Thursday too. The difference? Sunshine. A sunny day. The job had gone like cake. Sweet. Fast. A smooth getaway. They were singing. Money. Tons of it. No one got killed. Like cake. He didn't see the pushchair. Just the girl. His foot jerked too late, far too late. He saw her face. Saw it ashen. He sighed. He had missed her. Thank Christ! He had just missed her. Then he saw it, like a kite. Tumbling through the sky. The car squawking to a halt. The eyes. His. Hers. Through the glass. Her mouth. Open. Her eyes. So open. Hoops, loops of shocked blue. And out of the sky the baby tumbles. Jed heard it hit the roof. Not loud; but he heard it. He can hear it now. Then the scream reaches him through the windscreen that the baby is sliding down. Jed is wet with sweat. Then. Now. He stands forlornly and opens the door of the washing machine, pulls out the case. It is too heavy to take with him. He leans over and pushes it down the back.

Keeley was watching the news. It was an accident. Normally she didn't bother much. She'd been watching *Neighbours* and had just stayed sitting, too tired for some reason to get up and start her tea, when there he was, Carrow, in the same suit he'd taken off in her bedroom the last time he visited.

She'd started to listen to him; he was talking about a raid, looking straight into her eyes, as if talking just to her, when there was Jed and another man – well, photographs of them; half the screen each.

It was strange seeing two men she knew on the television. This is how it is for famous people, she thought. Friends, lovers, partners – they suddenly turn up on television in the very room you talk to them in. Famous people walk into a newsagent's and there's their photograph on the magazines, smiling down from the racks. It must be weird. She'd gone into Smith's recently and counted five magazines with pictures of Jamie Oliver on the front. She didn't buy any of them; he wasn't her type.

She understood that Jed was on the run; that Carrow's team were after him. She wondered if Jed's picture would be in the papers tomorrow.

And she knew both of them. More than knew them. She wished she had paid attention to the report from the beginning; she wanted more details. And she wondered if he might come to her, to hide. What would she do if he did? She heard Carrow warn viewers that Jed was armed, that he was dangerous and they shouldn't approach him. Dangerous. She thought how gentle he was with her; she had nothing to fear. It is funny how men can be – so tender when they are alone with a woman, so different out in the world. And sometimes the other way round.

The boss might send him to her, a sort of safe house. She couldn't refuse then, could she? Not that she would any-way, she thought. It would be nice if he came. Then as the item finished and the bulletin moved onto something about the railways the possibility occurred that if Jed came to her for a time, Carrow might also make one of his occasional visits. The thought alarmed her, but excited her too.

Andy Crawford sat impassively before the television listen-ing to Carrow. He already knew of course, had been in-formed within the hour. He looked at the pictures of Jed and Coy staring out blankly from the screen. Coy was OK; he'd had him safely housed in no time. They'd picked Darryl up, but he was safe. He knew the form; they'd get nothing from him. But where was Jed? And, more to the point, where was the caseload of fucking notes he'd lifted?

It was a bad day all right; Johnny Day dead, the job completely fucked up, and now it was looking as if Jed had done a stasher. No, surely not Jed? He'd been with him for years. A real receipt: totally reliable, even when he got lifted. You could always count on Jed. That's why he used him. He'd be in touch. It had only been a few hours after all. He'd be lying low for a bit. He'd be in touch. But why was his phone off? He'd tried a dozen times to reach him. The gun was a worry. His stomach turned – he didn't like it one little bit; too much was out of control. Sure, things go wrong on jobs, that's life, but if everyone does what they know they're supposed to, like Coy had done, then anything can be salvaged. Jed should have made contact. Immediately. He knew that. No, he didn't like the smell of this at all.

Jed was crouched under the canal bridge. His thighs ached. But not as much as his chest, his shoulder, his bloody neck. The whole area burned. He should stand up, move about, but he couldn't. He was transfixed by the calm band of unperturbed water before him. On either side of the bridge, the pocked surface of the canal bubbled beneath the rain's lash, like skin blistering.

Jed concentrated on the smooth surface, saw the curve of the bridge darkly reflected within it. He was trying to get his mind like that; become that calm band of water within the storm. Instead thoughts plopped and splattered, like large raindrops, one displacing another. What to do?

It was hopeless. Johnny Day was dead. He was sure of it. The job screwed. How many years was he looking at? You don't get away with it when something goes as wrong as this. Not even Black Andy could get him out of this one. It was hopeless. No! It wasn't! He had the money, hidden in the launderette. He had his gun too, here in his hand. He could ditch it now if he wished. Just whisk it away into the water. It'd be gone for ever. But no. That would destroy the calm, would be unlucky.

How had all this happened, he asked himself. What was he doing here? He knew the form, so why hadn't he contacted Crawford? What did he want? Money, he supposed, that's what he was in this game for. Well, he had got plenty of money now. He should ring the boss, report back; tell him the case of dosh was now stuffed behind a washing machine in the Mermaid Launderette. It wasn't too late; Crawford would tell him what to do. So, why was he crouching here beneath the bridge? Why didn't he get his phone out and ring? Exhaustion? A sort of paralysis? Or was this an opportunity? A chance to break away? Was he just trying to get up the balls to do a lifter?

Jed wanted to move, make something happen, but it meant surrendering his shelter and going out into the pitiless rain again. Further down the canal bank he could see the lights of the Little Moscow glimmering behind the sheets of rain. Perhaps he should go there.

Everything seemed to be fading away. He tried to recall faces: Johnny Day, Strombo, Crawford – Oh fuck! Crawford! He'd be going crazy. But he couldn't retrieve any of them. Faces he knew well, had seen that day – they were fading away from him, hidden behind the layers of rain, thick as time.

This was a dangerous place. Plenty of stories circulated in the Moscow of men who'd died under this bridge. Move, he told himself. Yelled it aloud, but the echo, after travelling the inner curve of the bridge, died away in the water and still he was motionless. Perhaps the ghosts of those dead men who had died here were holding him captive. Fuck! He didn't think like this.

He needed a drink – a stiff one. A whisky. Large. With a fag. Double heat.

He tried to get Keeley's face. He could describe it, but he couldn't see it. Not in her bed beneath him, an image he sometimes recalled when he was randy, not even in the white sunlight of that afternoon when he sent her child tumbling into the sky and out of life. He had lived with her frozen face of that day, like a newsflash stark before him; it had woken him a thousand times. Why couldn't he see her now?

Keeley took the newspapers from Mrs Nayer.

'You don't usually buy daily papers, Keeley.'

'No.' She didn't know what else to say.

'And three of them. They're all the same, you know.'

'It's just something to read.'

'Ah. You're a great reader, Keeley. I know that. Your magazines. I like reading too. But not these. Too depressing. I know the world is a bad place. I don't need to read about it. Sabre! Here! Sit down.' The dog had risen and started to move indolently towards Keeley. 'Sabre. Back here, I say.' The animal turned and returned to his position at the end of the counter. 'That's it. Good boy. He is very restless this morning, Keeley. I don't know why.'

There were pictures of Jed in two of the papers. The same picture that had been on the news last night: a mug-shot taken by the police when Jed had been arrested some time, like a passport picture.

Keeley didn't know what to do for the best – cut the pictures out, or keep the whole paper intact, as she did when Simon was killed. She wondered if she should have bought all of the papers, but that really would have made Mrs Nayer suspicious. Perhaps she would go to another shop later. But what if he came while she was out? She was sure he would come to her. She'd known him for ages. She couldn't believe it was him driving on that horrible day.

She hadn't seen him for a long time, but she recognized him. She had said nothing to the police. It had been an accident. But she wouldn't have shopped him, even if the Boss hadn't come to see her, given her money. She told Carrow she remembered nothing. He knew though. He showed her photographs. Jed was one of them. When they became close she admitted she knew Jed, from way back; if it had been him driving she would have recognized him. It wasn't because of the money. Right from the start she knew she wouldn't say anything.

When the bell rang the next day and she looked through the peephole, it was a face she didn't know. 'I'm Kieran. The Boss sent me.' He had an Irish accent, cropped hair, a nose ring – quite nice. She liked his fingernails – long and well shaped. A lovely pale pink. She'd been shocked by an article she'd read once about a top male model, gorgeous looking, who never allowed his hands to be photographed because he bit his nails. The article said it was due to pressure and insecurity. Keeley had always thought people like that were perfect, with great self-control. She'd never bit her nails and enjoyed painting them, filing them into shape.

Keeley led Kieran into the kitchen. 'The Boss wondered if you'd seen Jed? He's worried about him.'

'No. Not since a week last Monday. He brought some money round.'

'He's in bother, you see. Jed is. With the law. The Boss is worried about him. Wants to see he's all right.'

He handed her a piece of paper. Lined. A number written in blue Biro. 'He wants you to ring this number straightaway. The Boss does. If Jed comes round. OK? Immediately. Understand?'

'All right,' she said, taking the paper and fixing it to the fridge door with a magnet. Bart Simpson. She liked Bart.

She wasn't one for cartoons, but *The Simpsons* made her laugh sometimes.

Kieran gave her an envelope. 'Just a little extra. The Boss said. For expenses.'

'It's a bloody nightmare, I tell you.' Carrow is talking to Sean Dowd. Not exactly a mate, he used to be his boss. When Carrow needs to talk to someone these days Dowd is first choice. They're sitting over pints of lager, off patch, in the Popplewell, the only local in Birmingham that doesn't do lock-ins. Not surprising, Carrow thinks, looking round. Who'd want to spend more time in here than they had to?

'It seemed such a winner,' he said, returning to his melancholy theme. 'Easy. Just a quiet trip down the Smoke, and pick up.' He clicked his fingers to illustrate the simplicity of the exercise. 'Then those bastards of Crawford's have to get involved. And where are we? The Day kid dead and an enquiry on my hands that'll stuff promotion for months. Coy silent as a Trappist monk with a bad throat, and two men on the run. It's that bastard Owen I want. Soft as shit. Get him looking at twenty years and he'll leak enough to close the whole outfit down.'

'For a while.'

'That's good enough for me.'

'Still,' Dowd said thoughtfully, 'you've got a car boot full of gear, and you've got Strombo and Co.'

'Yeah. And they're all doing the mute. Cemetery silent. I tell you, the bloody KGB and their box of tricks wouldn't get anything out of them.'

'How's Old Man Day taking it?'

'Dunno. But you know that family, they think they're the Corleones.'

'So there'll be repercussions.'

Carrow gave a bitter laugh. 'Sure as JFK, mate.'

Dowd lifted his glass and took a drink. Carrow looked at him, totally out of place in this neighbourhood pub of jeans and tracksuit bottoms. How did he always manage to look so immaculate?

Dowd replaced his glass on the table. Took a cigarette and lit it. After exhaling, he leaned in closer to Carrow, risking his white shirt cuffs on the tabletop.

'It seems to me, Carra,' he said, 'that your intelligence is short. You should have known about the Crawford raid. They're tight, but not leak-proof.' Carrow nodded, he knew Dowd was right. 'You know as well as I do that the basis of this work is to get the info spot on; it's got to be right. Otherwise you get cock-ups like this.' Carrow winced at the word, *cock-up*. OK, it was a fair description, but he'd hoped for a bit of moral support from Dowd, that he'd tell him things weren't so bad. He should have known better. 'It's salvageable, though,' Dowd continued with certainty. 'But you've got to pick up the runners, and quick. Go for that Owen lad if he's the weak link.'

'Crawford will have him tucked up in bed by now.'

'Then find the bedroom.'

'Yeah. I wish.'

'Come on, Carra. There's going to be a fucking war going on in that camp. Nuclear. They fucked up big time. Crawford's not going to put up with that. If you haven't got a pokey there, which you should have, then find one, someone who knows what's going on. This is their moment of weakness, as well as yours.'

You needn't have added that last bit, Carrow thought, but still, Dowd was right as bloody always.

'She's gorgeous,' Dowd said, indicating the young barmaid collecting glasses who'd just passed their table. Carrow looked up. The girl was pretty all right: honey-coloured hair swept back into a cute tail, little black top bearing an appliquéd cherub leaving enough room for her narrow midriff to dazzle.

'Best thing about this pub,' Carrow said.

'Only good thing,' Dowd answered.

Trevor, the desk sergeant, waved Carrow across when he returned to the station. 'We've had a couple of calls I thought you should know about, sir.'

'Oh yeah?'

'Yes, sir. Both males. Both enquiring whether we have Jed Owens in custody. One claimed he was a journalist, but he was no journalist. Even the freebies wouldn't have him. The other said he was a friend. But I reckon it's Crawford's boys.'

'Sounds like it. Sounds like he's gone walkabout too.'

Jed's wet hair felt like a cap, plastered to his head. After leaving the shelter of the bridge, he'd trudged towards the Little Moscow sign. Its tawdry orange light, fighting the rain and the gathering darkness, offered no promise of hope, but still he was drawn. The dead water, attacked and ravaged by the rain, waited, patient as the past, to see what he would do.

He reached the bar and stood before its scarred door, but he could do no more. His hand wouldn't rise. He couldn't pull open the door, descend the stone steps, back into the world he knew.

'What the fuck is wrong with you?' he yelled into the weeping night. 'All you have to do is go in. Like a million other times. Walk down the steps. Stand at the bar. Nothing more. Crawford will know in minutes, and they'll be round for you.'

As he walked away from the Little Moscow, towards the threads of soft lights that were the streets and traffic of the city, he asked himself, What's wrong with being picked up by Crawford's men? It was normal procedure. It should have happened hours ago. They were his people. He was part of the tribe; always had been. It was his world. If you were loyal, Crawford looked after you. The way he'd treated Keeley proved that. No! He mustn't think about that. Not that. He had to try, instead, to understand what was happening to him. The one place he might be safe right now was the Little Moscow, yet he was walking away from it. He asked himself again what was happening to him, but there was nowhere, save the lights of the city ahead, to look for an answer.

Under one of the arches of the viaduct, huddled as if for shelter against the rain, was a Ka. A stupid pudding-shaped girls' motor. But it was wheels. Jed took it. Less than a minute and he was away, thankful that something had jerked him into action. He headed away from the city, towards the estates.

In his headlights he saw a question mark on the road before him, and instinctively swerved round the dead cat. He pulled into the Beechwood, a typical estate pub. The lounge was almost empty. Three lads played the fruit machine; a couple of teenagers were huddled into each other in the corner with glasses of Coke. A few old blokes sat at tables. He could hear noise from the bar; the football was on.

'You bin swimmin', darlin'?' The middle-aged barmaid laughed.

'Yeah. I came via the canal.' She was a short woman with a cheerfully lined plump face. Her shabby white cardigan had a pattern of cherries on it, and was misshapen where it was stretched to button across her bosom. Look more like apples than cherries round the chest area, Jed thought, or those things with the pips, fucking pomegranates. Jed ordered a lager, took out his cigarettes and laid them on the bar. SMOKING KILLS, the carton shouted at him in serious black print. He took a cigarette and lit it. Drew the smoke in. A screw of hot smoke, deep and sore. He exhaled. Beautiful.

Two blackboards were attached to the wall either side of the bar. One had the lunchtime menu chalked on it: sirloin and chips; chicken curry; chicken supreme; pensioners' specials. On the other board, chalked in ornate blue letters: ARE YOU A MILLIONAIRE? Underneath, more simply, in white: *Tonight's (Wed) Winning Numbers are, 8, 17, 24, 29, 40, 46.* One of them was his age, another his birthday. He only did the lottery on Saturdays. At the foot of the board, in pink balloon letters this time: *We Serve Champagne!* And a sketch of the tilted neck of a champagne bottle, its cork flying away from it.

Jed took his pint and cigarettes to a table. I'm like some sad old git, sitting alone in a poxy pub like this. But he couldn't think of anywhere else he wanted to be. The pain in his chest was easing. Just a throbbing tightness remained around his neck.

The young couple were kissing. Really going for it. The lads at the fruit machine laughed and two of the old guys started to play cards. From the bar a cheer. A goal had been scored.

The barmaid sneezed. 'Bless you,' the old guys chorused.

'It's these bleedin' flowers,' she said, sticking a tissue into her face, then indicating an elaborate arrangement of artificial flowers in a basket at the end of the bar. 'They need a bleedin' good dust.'

'Chuckin' out, more like,' an old fellow sitting alone called out. 'They've been there since I was a lad.'

'Sod this,' Jed muttered to himself. He downed his pint, stubbed his cigarette and was up and away, though where the fuck to, he had no idea.

'Night, love,' the barmaid called. 'Watch out for the canal.'

*

Keeley poured bleach into the toilet bowl. Colourless liquid, clear as water, but deadly poisonous. At school they had read a book about a girl who killed herself by swallowing bleach. 'Burnt her insides out.' She remembered the words.

She looked around the bathroom; everything shone. She smiled. She was proud of how she kept her flat. It was all those years living with Gran. She was spotless, that woman was. She used to complain about Keeley when she was a kid, a teenager. 'Dirty little pro,' she called her. Keeley smiled. She had been a bit wild when she was young. But she thought the world of her really, her Gran did, do anything for her. She yelled a lot when Keeley got pregnant and cried a bit; disappointment, she said it was. Her nerves were always bad. But she was there for her. No question about it. A heart of gold that woman. Then she died.

When the bell rang Keeley knew it was him. She was in her blue negligée, just lying on the bed reading her horoscope in *M Girl* (it was always the best) and listening to music from the radio. Behind the music the clatter of rain battering the window.

He looked terrible and, because of that, he looked in some way wonderful. The wet, stubbled face; the rain-slicked hair. The grey eyes, not empty, but on a low light.

'I'm sorry, Keel,' he said. His voice sounded unfamiliar; as rain-damaged as the rest of him. 'The state I'm in. I'm in a bit of trouble. Will you do me a favour?'

'It's OK,' she said. 'I hoped you'd come. I've seen you on telly.'

He was sleeping when she left the bed. His shuddering fitfulness was childlike; the gasps for breath as if he were going under water. In the kitchen she looked out at the lights of the city. She felt special. He'd come as she predicted. She realized now that it had been a certainty. Just as now she was certain the other one would come too. It was destiny. Tonight Jed had done her better than ever before, really worked at it, she could tell. And that pleased her too. He will have to stay. He will be here when the other one comes. And she gazed at the lovely threads of light smeared like snail-trails inside the rain.

When Jed woke the bed was empty. A shoal of memories returned. But he wanted Keeley, and his desire kept all else at bay. The sex they'd had just a few hours before had been rough, and he was surprised – by himself; by her. So, she liked it rough. And he'd always been so gentle before.

Then thoughts of the boss, Black Andy, Mad Andy, pushed hard at the barrier of his lust – how the hell had he got himself into this shit? So quickly. Was it the money? Was he a lifter, after all? No, it didn't feel like that. It was to do with Keeley, and what he had done that sunny day. He got out of bed. She was standing in the kitchen in the dark. Looking out the window. Silhouetted by the faint, dismal light from the city. She knew he was walking towards her, but didn't move until she felt the gun on her neck. His free hand took her buttock. Just breathing for a while, both of them, looking out at the estate and breathing. 'Bend over. Put your mouth on the windowsill.' He must have felt this desperate, this horny, this urgent, before – but if so, he couldn't remember it.

He wasn't a brute, though. He was only acting, exciting her, and after the driving entry and the initial thrusts he wept and eased her forward into a complete curve, like a seahorse, so his tongue could nuzzle in the spaces between the pebbles of her spine. 'Keel. Keel. You're a star. You are. You're a fuckin' star.' And, as he put the gun down by the sink so he could use both hands to caress her neck, there was the inkling of a belief that he might never need it again. Then all thought was lost again as he drove them towards climax: arms and legs quivering like tentacles, eyes fixed ahead to the window and what swam beyond it.

Later, as Jed lay lost in sleep with Keeley lying wakeful in his arms, the idea came to her. This was her moment. She'd read about other women who had used this phrase. A life-changing opportunity. Jed was in the newspapers, had been on television. So had Carrow. When he came to her, as she knew he must, she would have both of them. Soon, she was convinced, Carrow would lie beside her here just as Jed lay beside her now. She was like a lure that drew these two men towards her; had been for ages really. Jed's gun was in the fridge. She'd offer Jed to Carrow. She'd never shopped anyone in her life before, but now: *this is my moment; what can I do?* His arrest would be in the papers, on the news, and she – she had the story: the lover of the cop and the criminal. It would mean shopping Carrow too, in a way, she supposed – the newspapers would want all the intimate details. She recalled articles about women with similar stories to tell; they were always photographed glamorously, provocatively. Fame beckoned and Keeley selected outfits for photocalls and press conferences as she drifted into sleep.

The hot water washed over Carrow, sluicing away shampoo and filling the bathroom with steam. Behind the roar of water Eddie Grant sang 'Electric Avenue' from the other room. Carrow reached round the shower curtain and pulled a warm towel from the rack. He felt energized, excited as he vigorously dried himself. Like putting a lot of money on the roulette wheel at the casino. It might take some time to make your choice, but once the decision was made, once the dough was down, all you could do was wait for the result. This was like that. He'd decided she must know. Owen must have been there. Crawford's lot were in a real spin, making silly mistakes in their efforts to track him down, not like that crew at all. Phone calls to the law, for Christ's sake. Owen had obviously lifted the takings and was on the run. Carrow just knew he'd be in touch with Keeley, was sure of it; she was the key.

So. Shower. Clean boxers. Tasty aftershave. Expensive gear, that always impressed her. A couple of rubbers slipped into his jacket pocket, and he was away. This was business, sure, but it could be pleasure too. She was a sweet woman, a very pretty one. And a fucking good shag. He knew he was on the home run.

It had taken some time – well, he needed to recover. For a whole day he said nothing really except please and thank you. Then. The rain stopped. A pale sunlight filled the lounge. And sitting in the armchair, Keeley curled up on the sofa opposite, he talked to her – about the raid, about the money in the Mermaid Launderette, about other things he'd done in his life. Keeley listened and watched the light return to his eyes as he talked. Like Oprah Winfrey, she thought. Then, no. More like I'm a journalist collecting a story – which in a way she was.

She liked him like this. Quiet. Gentle again. It was exciting to have seen his other side, the side he used to do all the things he was telling her about, but a side which as he sat in this lovely room with her seemed to have dissolved away, like stains out of dirty washing, she thought, and giggled.

'What you laughin' at?'

'Nothin'. Well, you. You're funny. Nice funny. All the different bits to you.'

He rose and came to sit beside her, put his arm round her, so he could feel her hair against his cheek. So close, she'd have noticed if he had tensed when she told him about Carrow, or if his breathing had changed. But neither of these things happened.

'Don't worry,' she said. 'When he comes I'll act just like normal. He'll see you're not here.' And when the talking stopped they both looked out through the window into the clear pale sky. Though Jed felt safe here with her in his arms, the empty sky was no comfort; he knew he could, at any moment, tumble from it into the chaos he was trying to escape. For Keeley, the empty blue was a familiar place; like being in a plane, she often thought, though she'd never been in one. You need never look down. Down doesn't exist.

Fat Alex stood behind the bar of the Little Moscow. He didn't like this. Andy Crawford and two of his blokes sat in the first alcove where they could see everyone coming down the stairs. Staring. Assessing. Fuck, this place held the answers to a lot of questions it was better not to ask, but not, he was sure, to the whereabouts of Jed Owen and, more to the point, Strombo's money. Crawford's money now, he supposed. Shit, it looked like it was Owen's, at least for now. All Alex needed was for the Doberman Crew to turn up, and Christ knows what would happen. Well, no. It wasn't just Christ; anybody with a brain half the size of a dead fish's would know, and Fat Alex shuddered at the thought.

No one had put the jukebox on. No one was playing snooker. There was plenty of booze going down, but no one was getting drunk. It felt like being in church, or court.

When Crawford's mobile went Alex jumped. And he was pretty sure everyone else did too.

'Oh fuck,' he thought, 'I hope this is good news.'

Sometimes you just know when something is right. You know you're backing the right horse. Carrow was near hard with anticipation as he pulled up outside Walton Towers. Thank fuck the rain had stopped. He alarmed the car. Went into the rabbit-hutch of a shop at the bottom of the tower for some mints to sweeten the breath. The shop smelt of dog and curry. The woman behind the counter was eating a late lunch. Three p.m. Mid-afternoon. Always a nice time for a spot of relaxed shagging. That's the way he'd play it – nice and easy, slow and tender, gentle.

Water was dripping down the walls of the stairwell. Great maps of oozing dampness like a mythological disease at the heart of the building. Shit, how the hell did those walls get in such a state? They were inner walls. But at least the bloody kids weren't around.

This is my moment, Keeley thought as she looked at Carrow's face through the peephole. Handsome and smiling. Confident. Not like Jed. Like the old Jed, a bit. But not like the new one. The one she had been with for the last two days.

She'd put him in Simon's room, which spooked him. But she was determined. Stay here. He knows I never unlock this room. Trust me. He wished it were night so he didn't have to look at the pictures, the toys. They weren't making much noise. He'd heard a bit of a yell, which he presumed was Carrow shooting his load, not much from her. Not like this morning. He could hear a few words now; they were talking.

When eventually Carrow asked her if she'd heard anything from Jed Owen she was turned against him. His arms around her chest, her arse tucked into his crotch. Comfy. 'Oh yes,' she said, 'he's here. In the other room.' In the shock of her words Carrow's arms loosed their hold and Keeley slipped out of his grasp and out of the bed. She took her kimono robe and put it on, smiling at Carrow as he attempted to sit upright, or get out of bed. Neither of them was sure which. 'He's in the other room,' she repeated. 'Look.'

And she opened the bedroom door and then the door opposite to Simon's room. Carrow and Jed looked at each other, both mute, both struggling with the instinct to swift movement that the sight of the other provoked. And then, for Keeley, as she looked from one man to the other, and felt wonderful in a way she had only dreamed she one day might, the script changed.

'You see,' she said to Carrow, 'he's here, has been for over a week. Here with me. In that bed mostly, where you are.' She watched Carrow's eyes widen, his mouth open as if he were about to sing. 'Then the other day. When we saw everything on telly. He was scared to death.' Carrow reared up bare-chested in the bed, looked at the man across the hallway. The getaway man, who drove cars like a lunatic, killed people with them. He looked different.

'Then I told him about you. How kind you are to me. How good you were to me about Simon, when you came round for statements.' She laughed lightly. She knew now that her story would never be told in the Sundays; no cram of photographers, no flashlights. Her story would never be filmed, but if it had been, then Victoria Beckham should play her part. She felt like Victoria, standing here. A strong woman. She seized her opportunities. Or Cate Blanchett – turning every negative into a positive. She laughed again.

'Of course, Jed was a bit suspicious. Anyone would be. Policeman investigating a child's death sleeping with the mother, visiting her on duty. At all hours of the day and night. Sounds like he was taking advantage, Jed said. Abusing his position.' She lifted Carrow's boxer shorts from the floor and sat on the bed beside him. 'But I explained. Carrow's not like that. He's a decent bloke. Ambitious, yes, but decent. Once he knows you've been here with me all the time. The only time I've left the flat was this morning, for a couple of hours. I had to go to the launderette. You know I like to keep everything clean. Once he knows you were here with me when that raid took place, I said. Once he understands. Everything will be OK.' She held out the shorts to Carrow. 'Would you like a bit of privacy to get dressed?'

Something had changed. Alex could tell. Just from the expression on Crawford's face.

'You're a star, love. I'll send Kieran round. For the laundry. Tell the lad to look after hisself. Give me a call when he's feelin' better.' He clicked off and pocketed his phone. 'Fuckin' beaut. It was that Keeley tart,' he explained to the men beside him who, seeing his change of mood, were beginning to relax. 'She's got him. Owen. Bin there all the time. And the money. Seems he 'ad some sort of breakdown. Went round in a terrible state. Kept telling 'er to get the money to me, get in touch with me, but she couldn't get the number out of him. Then she remembers it was on the fridge all the time. Bloody good woman that one. Don't think we'll be usin' Jed for a while, though. Kieran. You know the place. Go round and collect. And look after 'er. A grand, I think.'

He was gentle again. He liked it like this as much as she did. He smiled down at her. That smile was lovely, she thought. This was lovely. He was good; knew just how to get her ready, knew just when she was ready. He had the condom sachet between his teeth, starting to tear at it through a wide grin. 'No.' She reached up and took the rubber from his hand. 'You won't be needing these any more.'

H P Tinker

H P TINKER was born in Southport in 1969 and now lives in Manchester, where he has carved a niche for himself as the 'Thomas Pynchon of Chorlton-cum-Hardy'. His short fiction has appeared in *Ambit*, *Pulp.net* and *3am Magazine*, and many other highly obscure places. For more information you can visit him at www.hptinker.co.uk

The Shattered Window

H P Tinker

Williams and Enklemann are investigating the reported breaking of a large plate-glass window in a house on Elizabeth Street. Discovery of the shattered window followed a report of a possible burglary at 2:29 a.m. yesterday. Williams and Enklemann enter the building through the broken window to check for suspects; inside, finding the dead body of a young man and, next to him, a bird with a broken neck. Williams and Enklemann later conclude that no entry by another party has been gained. The cause of death is unknown. Initially, they begin talking to people who may possibly have been present at the time of the alleged incident or else were in the general vicinity at the time of the alleged incident or else have something potentially enlightening to say about a related matter that might possibly prove of some significance in the long term to the alleged incident.

'I don't understand, I don't understand it at all,' says a neighbour with blank eyes.

'That's perfectly OK,' say Williams and Enklemann. 'We barely understand it ourselves . . .'

Newspaper clippings, photographs, photocopies, magazines; information, shards of information, slivers of information, daggers of information. Williams and Enklemann flicking rapidly, haphazardly, through the newspapers, people vanishing all the time, it seems: failing to return home, disappearing from hotel rooms, abandoning cars in unlikely locations, not arriving for their own marriage ceremonies, failing to show up generally. All the available information tends to confirm the initial impression that life is a series of people disappearing all the time . . .

Williams and Enklemann speak to a woman: a skeletal frame in a geometric print dress, baffling black hair, vintage shades: 'I am a very weak woman and do not have the strength to speak for long . . . I'm seriously troubled by serious decline . . . My husband went missing . . . Vanished from the face of the earth . . . They looked . . . Then they stopped looking . . . Nobody is looking any more . . . I haven't set eyes on him for quite some time . . . I do not want you to find him again . . . I hope he never comes back . . . Please can you make sure he never comes back?'

Williams and Enklemann receive a mysterious package in the post, an unmarked video tape.

On first viewing, it is extraordinary: bizarre CCTV footage, jerky hand-held camcorder shots zooming in and out on a young couple, a man and a woman, spliced together in a Jarmanesque patchwork of blurry black and white shopfronts, Super-8 close-ups, elaborate Hollywood tracking shots. Climbing out of a beige cab. Visiting the Museum of Comparative Zoology. Eating at Albie Singer's, a Yiddish café, traditional Ashkenazi cuisine: hallah bread, gefilte fish, chopped liver, pickled beef, goose prosciutto, lokshen kugel, shiny honey cake. Tripping down the neon-blazing red-light streets, waving cruelly at the rubber-coated women in the windows, a woman in a dark khaki leather jacket, feathered vest, short black cotton skirt; oddly casual: burgundy leather boot-kicks, diagonal print polo.

Climbing into a beige cab, interior footage now: her golden hair everywhere, arms wrapped around each other, almost . . . almost . . . almost smiling towards the camera, slightly too close, faces unfocused. Then freeze-frame bedroom footage: undressed, pressed together in ten-gallon hats, her on top, him trapped in a hat, expressions of contortion, blanched by the glare of amateur lighting, looking young, unlined, unworn by time and awkward events and unexpected deaths and unwanted twists of fate, eyes gleaming with life and life yet to be lived and things yet to happen, gazing beyond the camera lens to some unseen vantage point, some long-forgotten reverse angle, some long-lost, unremembered moment of vanished youth, vanquished dreams and vapid designs . . .

On subsequent viewings, however, Williams and Enklemann find it appears to be blank.

Williams and Enklemann standing on a platform, alone, sharing a wan expression. The end of the platform feels like the end of the world. People glancing at them. They toy with their holsters, nervously.

Williams and Enklemann interview a leading avant-garde nuclear theorist with a terrifying capacity to digress:

'. . . of course, sausage is the worst offender in the meat world. One sausage can contain meat from one thousand cows. It's the ground-up spinal cord and brain in the sausage that transmit the disease, although I wouldn't wish to eat any part of a dead mad cow. Mad cow disease is *very* difficult to kill. It is spread by twisted rogue proteins called prions, which then mutate other proteins in their image. The rogue prion that appears to cause BSE and associated diseases has a particular shape. When these misshapen prions are activated they begin to convert the other prions around them. The incubation time is very long in this disease. One documentary I saw showed chickens being fed a mix of ground-up male chicks, plus their own faeces, which had been boiled and infused with antibiotics and vitamins. Well, what do you expect from corporate factory farms? Remember, the corporation derives from one core 'principle': do whatever it takes to make as much profit as quickly as possible . . .'

Over the course of twenty-four hours' intensive questioning, he reveals nothing of use.

Williams and Enklemann sleep, but never dream.

Williams and Enklemann in a heavily crowded non-smoking carriage, gripped by an addiction to the melancholy of solitary travel through the cold dark cities of the world, surrounded by deafening schoolgirls and suddenly aware of being entangled in a world of investigation: a world of surprising nuisances and revelations, a world of unconvincing policemen and imaginary information, a world of fake guns and alibis loaded with intent, a world of drug-dealing drug dealers, dragged-up drag queens, cheerless cheerleaders, middle-class ladies in cement . . . a potential world . . . potentially littered with a handful of blondes, wisecracking, sassy and foul-mouthed . . . a world that once entered might prove difficult to be successfully extricated from . . .

Williams and Enklemann eating dinner with a series of deftly timed fork movements. Not fully engaged with the meal, the process of eating. Later, Williams and Enklemann recollecting little about it. Tomorrow, probably having no memory of the meal occurring whatsoever . . . thinking about the investigation and the course of the investigation . . . writing a list of questions to ask people in the latter stages of the investigation. Looking down: two empty plates staring back at them – the meal finished, apparently.

A mysterious pair of bloodstained hot pants is discovered in a sand dune, all the initial tension of the investigation dissipating as more and more clues are slowly revealed . . .

Williams and Enklemann in a hotel room, watching a blue movie together: real people really fucking real people . . . opening an attaché case . . . contemplating the contents of the opened attaché case alone . . . Williams alone in the bathroom for a moment, deciding to grow a beard in response to the mounting sense of frustration he feels.

Williams and Enklemann walking into a basement and discovering a torture victim tied to a metal bed. Seeing the man having his head bludgeoned twenty-two times with a fire extinguisher . . . seeing a man being bludgeoned twenty-two times on the head with a fire extinguisher is one of life's more sobering incidents, it occurs to Williams and Enklemann afterwards.

Williams and Enklemann, now genuinely appalled by the Mexican-style corruption being uncovered in this investigation, flounder in a sea of worthless information, violence, porn, chloroform, poppers and a ballet dancer who fell into a vegetative state. Williams and Enklemann feeling like Django Reinhardt undoubtedly must have felt . . . at some point . . . in his life.

Williams and Enklemann off-duty: talking to tall girls in tall clothes, entering rooms, leaving them again, glancing up at ceilings, hearing sentences that signify nothing, later being beguiled by those very sentences, sentences that signify nothing of great import, rising from chairs, sitting back down again, spreading mirth generously across South East Asian faces . . .

Williams and Enklemann involved in a tragic accident with a minibus carrying a jazz quartet. Williams escapes unscathed, Enklemann dies at the scene, but the jazz quartet use the event as a motivational force to make more proficient use of their rhythm section.

At night, alone, Williams tortures himself with visions of Enklemann crossing the room: Enklemann crossing the room with some swagger, Enklemann traversing a length of carpet between a door and a bar, a zone of such rich promise, ripe with possible sex, body odours, surprising new affections . . . Crossing rooms was nothing to Enklemann. To Enklemann, crossing rooms was almost second nature, came quite naturally really.

Enklemann was good at crossing rooms.

Williams tries to distract himself by finding other things to do, listening to Ron Sexsmith and Diana Krall and Richard Strauss and Craig David, finding the delicate piano figures, the clarity and subtlety, the honey-dipped vocals, the pre-programmed beats, the dreamily soporific *mis-en-scène* emerge with credibility only half intact, nothing inspiring him, nothing forcing itself hummingly through the surface of things, the pop-induced rancour, the bitterness of the singer-songwriter . . .

Williams turns on the TV. There's a programme about Addis Ababa in which a housewife has an infected anus. Williams changes channels. An operation is in progress, a doctor prodding about in somebody's intestines. Williams turns over again. A documentary about lighthouses. Williams turns over again. A woman is being sawn in half by a magician with jug-handle ears. Williams turns over again. Fat men are wrestling in front of an enormous crowd, something Williams can't see any value in.

Where is my guilt-ridden sidekick? thinks Williams.

Williams decides to leave the house.

In a noodle bar Williams lifts a glass of Czech beer from a plain wooden table and toasts Enklemann. In the glass he sees his own reflection, himself looking like Vincent van

Gogh with a mop of Ramones hair, in tight blue jeans, his time-honoured punk jacket festooned with badges. Williams feels lost without Enklemann, lost in this place. Seeing a woman in a long red leather jacket, with thick-soled black boots, red lips, black hair, leaning against a wall, smoking casually, with an ice-cream resolve. A smile passing across her mouth, briefly. And white socks everywhere, worn with shorts, the white socks pushed down in an amateur porn way, like Emilio Estevez in *The Breakfast Club*. There's an eighties-flavoured techno beat too: dark, chaotic, aggressive, grimy. Williams feeling like a battle-scarred Vietnam vet listening to civilians talking about the hard day they just had at the office. Flossy glossy miniskirts hitched up all around him. Hair and the illusion of hair: suburban haircuts, eyes shielded by heavy fringes, car coats, donkey jackets, multi-pocketed workman's jackets, corduroy pants tucked into steel toe-capped boots, quilted bomber jackets unzipped from cuff to elbow, black satin shell suits, safari jackets, collarless granddad shirts, painter's trousers, dinner jackets cut into waistcoats. Next to Williams at the bar, a man sporting only a luxuriant moustache, wraparound sunglasses and a pair of underpants who claims to be recording an album of Dean Martin covers for charity.

'Men fight. Men are ugly. Men are stupid and selfish lovers,' somebody else says behind him . . .

Williams finishes his drink, a diet Coke, asking for another. He asks for ice and lemon to be added to the diet Coke. Next time, asking bourbon to be added to the diet Coke and ice and lemon. Next time, skipping the diet Coke. Next time, skipping the ice and lemon. Williams telling someone next to him: 'Sometimes the world can look a lot more complex than it really is . . .'

The tall European has a look of surprise on their face. They seem unconvinced.

Expelling urine into a grey urinal, Williams is thinking

about calling a cab, perhaps entering the city, perhaps not. Thinking: *If things happen for a reason that nobody can understand, why should anyone make any attempt to understand them?*

Outside: there is a city on fire, seething with ideas, punchy choruses and heavy guitar lines. Williams feeling a little disturbed . . . a woman passing him in the street, walking straight past him, not veering, his mother, or the image of mother, not veering, the same eyes, nose, hair, smile, teeth, mother no longer dead, five feet in front, less than five feet in front, opening her mouth, smiling, as if about to speak, as if to say hello. Reality stabbing at his temples. Williams wondering what this has got to do with anything anyway, wondering what is happening here, no memory of past events, no sequence, successfully blocked out perhaps, only an absence in his head, a space where these events should be . . .

Williams noting how sometimes the past can be fairly difficult to cope with.

Down in the subway, Williams sees a woman in distress, an assailant attempting to grapple her to the ground. These events are lucid to Williams, more lucid than any in recent memory. Will they, as seems certain, spiral inevitably out of control and lead inexorably to a sustained and repeated nine-minute rape ordeal? (Williams intervenes: repeatedly striking the man in the face with a rolled-up copy of the *Times Educational Supplement*, a useful weapon in unlikely circumstances.)

This woman, she has a high, determined forehead, Hollywood eyebrows, full Elvis lips, straight hair cut tight to the chin. She is wearing a tight sweater, hot pants and a denim jacket. On her feet is a pair of worn-out trainers, soles hanging off, over her shoulder a tatty bag slung like a sack.

She has two deep-set black eyes.

'How can I thank you?' she says.

'Actually, I can think of any number of ways.'

She bites into a pear. 'I can take you somewhere. I can show you something. Do you want to go somewhere? Do you want to see something?'

'Possibly. Maybe you could throw me a few spare details?'

She bites into the pear again and snorts. 'Life's too short for details. What do you need details for? All you need is the bigger picture . . .'

Then she finishes the pear.

At the top of the subway, Williams finds an unchained bicycle, a cheap child's bicycle, which strikes him as a poetic enough image of escape. Without speaking, they begin pedalling away, the saddle wobbling, her doing most of the pedalling at the front, Williams behind, legs wrapped furiously around her back . . .

Her apartment is mauve.

The walls are mauve. The sofa is mauve. Everything is more or less mauve. (Williams wondering: *What exactly is the meaning of all this mauve?*) She is a luminous and intoxicating creature, perfectly relaxed in the company of others, perfectly relaxed in her own nakedness, parting her clitoris with her fingers . . . Williams wondering: *Can you part a clitoris?* . . . penetrating her feeling as if he's penetrating some deep dark secret code. Williams finds sleeping with her to be an oddly rewarding experience. One moment she is afraid, the next ecstatic, the next horrified, the next utterly amiable.

She also supplies her own narration:

'. . . when I was a young girl, twelve approximately, my mother moved us away from our father, from a small town to another small town slightly larger than the first. I was unhappy and experienced my first bout of depression then . . . which basically lasted until I was about twenty-four . . .'

'Fate has brought us together like this . . .' she tells Williams, later, before collapsing.

That night Williams dreams of waking in a bare room inside a large red-brick tower, there being nothing in the room except for a high window. Somehow he is able to reach up to the window but is unable to see through the window, or guess at what is on the other side.

Williams makes a decision.

Shattering the window with an angled elbow, smashing it into several easy pieces . . . tiny pieces of shattered window falling like diamonds . . . the breeze from the shattered window invigorating . . . Finally Williams can see through the glass he has shattered and out of the tower: past solemn heads of stone-faced gargoyles, through sheaves of ivy, to a beautiful sun-drenched garden below. Through the shattered window Williams sees many things, the beauty of the outside world being far more colourful than he had initially anticipated . . .

Epilogue:

So, this is why people shatter windows, Williams realizes the next day, analysing his dream. The shattering of a window, any window, is heavily symbolic and resonates through your life. The shattering of a window can be seen as the breaking of one man's heart and/or his breakthrough into another world. The gargoyles on the walls might be some intractable depression or the forces of containment. The ivy outside? That must be generally indicative of finding new love . . . and the sun-drenched garden must represent the possibility of finding that love in the unlikeliest of places and the entirely unexpected possibility of a brightly lit future yet to come . . .

City of Women

H P Tinker

On Tuesday night two of my officers shot and killed a deaf mute who they said was 'menacing' them with a garden rake. Afterwards, according to several eyewitnesses, they appeared 'nonchalant' and 'stood around' laughing and telling jokes. Under questioning, they claimed they only fired when the man swung the rake at them 'crazily'. They claimed they did not know the man was a deaf mute. They claimed he was 'wearing a hat' at the time of the incident. In my view, they behaved professionally, without reproach. In some cases, you see, there has been the suggestion of a hat.

In other cases, however, there has not.

No, we are no longer popular in this city of ours.

Statistics show that my officers kill citizens at a higher rate than any other officers in the country. We have a rate of 0.92 fatal shootings per 100,000 residents, plus other general killings, widespread frame-ups and various minor acts of brutality. Recently, a series of sickening phone calls has been sickening me. Now I am fighting just to get all this sickness out of my system.

People keep telling me sickening things.

'Get out of this city,' these sick voices say. 'You must haul your godforsaken ass away from the cheap perfume. You must haul yourself away from the sickness . . . you must haul your godforsaken sick ass out of here . . .'

Then they hang up unhelpfully.

In all cases, the voices sound uncannily like my late mother's. Is somebody trying to tell me something? I wonder, pulling into a motorway service station much later, the Human League's 'Love Action' unexpectedly on the radio . . .

'Another suicide?' somebody asks me from behind.

'Yes,' I mumble, not turning around, a little embarrassed. Spontaneous female suicides have been erupting across the city like a kind of sociological sickness.

'We are investigating every possible connection . . .' I tell people, studying another corpse, near Knutsford, another dead woman. Somehow she has managed to stab and butcher herself thoroughly with a long knife. And then inserted a child's pistol inside herself. *But why?*

Her jawbone is missing, too, though this isn't regarded with undue suspicion.

'Noleen Hertz was a remarkably talented lady,' I tell TV reporters outside the crime scene. 'When dealing with the suicide of a remarkably talented lady, I've found that almost anything is possible . . .'

The Norleen Hertz case shares several similarities with other unsolved suicides in the files.

'There are similarities,' I tell a crowd of people inside the Disney Shop, 'with the famous random self-slashing of Claudia Finkle on 15 November 1998. The main similarity is the knife wounds. Without drawing any conclusions, it appears that today's victim stabbed herself several times before slitting her own throat . . .'

People tell me they are worried by the imaginative suicide of manicurist Rita Barker, 53, from Crumpsall. She created an elaborate system of weights and pulleys and crushed herself beneath a block of frozen tiramisu. They ask me what we are doing about it.

'We are doing what investigators do,' I tell them. 'We are tall and have an imposing presence. In this case, the manner of death clearly indicates that there was a serious attempt on behalf of manicurist Rita Barker, 53, from Crumpsall, to deliberately kill herself and we intend to do something about these facts very shortly . . .'

But time drags.

There are more suicides.

Several have aroused our curiosity, much like girls dawdling on street corners in thin cotton dresses. One woman is found curled in a foetal position, wearing a chocolate brown jogging suit: Sylvia Sleep, 67, who spontaneously committed suicide in Fallowfield whilst putting the bin out early Thursday morning. She apparently blew herself up with a homemade explosive device, fitted inside her girdle. Various of her internal organs have since turned up in an experimental BBC4 ballet, which received widespread plaudits.

'Why this occurred, we simply don't know,' I inform the press, sheepishly. 'Yes, we are appealing to the public to start drawing some conclusions for us . . .'

Absolute shock and initial confusion have since given way to a greater sense of shock and some even larger confusion.

'One by one our women are being brutally taken from us,' one man told me, a fantasy-driven Quorn salesman from Withington. 'Personally, I don't think that's quite right. I only have two great-granddaughters. Soon I won't have any.'

We understand the public's concern. We are currently investigating a number of trash cans put out particularly early every Tuesday morning by particularly suspicious residents.

'What do we do now?' my team asks.

'Pardon?' I reply, not listening.

'What do we do now?' my team asks again.

'We do what all good investigators do,' I tell them, feeling like I'm in a Lars von Trier musical and about to burst into song.

'What do all good investigators do?' my team asks.

But I don't answer. I don't burst into song. I pull a facial expression, the meaning of which I don't understand.

'I wish I could tell you that we are investigating every possible connection,' I inform my superiors at the annual policemen's ball. We are midway into the second act: a band of tiny Elvises performing some of his greatest hits in Ancient Sumerian. But in actual fact we are not. In all honesty, we are actually being pretty lax in that regard. I must admit, though, I am enjoying the case and that shocks me. There's a thin line between crime and pleasure . . . and it is absolutely wrong to confuse the two.

More bodies.

Three hanging from the ceiling of a Chorlton tanning centre. Like abattoir carcasses in a challenging YBA installation. Spinning in a serene, prescriptive motion. We identify the bodies as three women. Their names? Tallulah Copeland. Felicia Baez. Hermione Blue. All thought-provokingly six foot tall, of slender build. Who were they, these women? Why would they want to hang themselves from the ceiling like that? What would be their motive for being up there? The tanning centre was not burgled, but there was an appointment booked for a mystery customer at about eleven a.m. No money was missing from the victims' handbags, although their ages – two elderly, one middle-aged – may, or may not, prove significant.

'Some sort of pact?' somebody behind me suggests. 'Like the Sammy Davis Jnr incident?'

'Maybe,' I mutter.

We never have successfully concluded whether the Sammy Davis Jnr incident stemmed from a simple sequence of chance events or . . . something else. We have taken calls (many of an obscene nature) from around the UK and the United States and followed thousands of leads in the years since the incident. All for nothing.

'Yes, there are similarities,' I tell some women I know, former secretaries of mine. 'But we are not drawing any conclusions. We can't. We haven't any to draw at the moment . . .'

Kitty Goldsmith, the young woman who found the three bodies at the Chorlton tanning centre, also called the authorities, having arrived for an appointment at about eleven fifteen a.m. In an entirely unrelated incident, she had only just been sexually assaulted in front of the salon by a close family friend. In the small, harshly lit interrogation room it transpires she is a keen collector of secondhand jigsaw puzzles.

Her motive for doing such a thing remains unclear.

On GMR this morning: Ralph Schmidt, 79, owner of one of the unluckiest faces in Britain, who lives across the street from the salon: 'The investigator came by again this morning and said he didn't know any more now than he did right after it happened . . .'

Not feeling myself after seeing the item, feeling my teeth and my fists and my buttocks clench, feeling an expression pulling hard on my face, an expression I last experienced in the company of three semi-naked women. *What's the matter with my heart? Why is it so steadfastly refusing to open? Why is it always so heavy?*

'What I fear most is the dark nature of the connection between these deaths . . .' I confess in a corner of the Cornerhouse, clutching a Bud Light, a Brie sandwich and a rolled-up copy of the *TV Times*.

There is one connection between the suicides, it seems: all the victims were known to have had legs like Cyd Charisse. The victims all arrived expecting an appointment with a trained masseur, we have learned, an expert in the treatment of older women with legs like Cyd Charisse. We are interviewing all known convenience shop assistants who have legs like Cyd Charisse. We are examining their legs very closely. One woman, Mabel Mannering, describes travelling to see *The Marriage of Figaro* in the Bristol area at the time of the deaths. The revue passed off without incident. 'A good time was had by all,' Mannering recalls.

We are sweeping the general public for information. We interview Ralph Schmidt, 79, without good reason. We interview the friends and family of Tallulah Copeland, Felicia Baez and Hermione Blue, who clearly don't know anything. We'd like to interview Cyd Charisse for the sheer hell of it. Some people want to be interviewed, it seems. They state they put their trash cans out particularly early every Tuesday morning when in fact they don't. Normally, under routine questioning, they break fairly quickly and speak candidly about their motivations for doing so. We interview Ralph Schmidt, 79, again – again without good reason. We pull him in for questioning early Sunday morning, hoping to catch him out. 'I wish I could tell you something,' says Ralph Schmidt, 79, who still lives across the street from all the initial shock and confusion. 'I wish I could have seen more, but I didn't. I am partially sighted.'

'Absolutely, we're concerned,' I tell the press, who have gathered outside the latest crime scene with their microphones. 'I used to have legs like Cyd Charisse myself. My wife still does, as it happens. Their shapeliness is often commented upon. So naturally there is some concern in our household.' (But why do they feel the need to do that? Gather outside the crime scene with their microphones? *Why do they gather like that*? What precisely does it achieve?)

There is one new lead: a top hat, found outside the Trafford Centre.

A sighting of a man might also prove significant. We believe that this man walked into the salon in a chequered suit and bowler hat. Another sixty-two witnesses described seeing the same person 'loitering' in Didsbury. (In the detective world, people who loiter are always regarded with the utmost suspicion.)

Now I am failing. I fail. I have failed. I study photographs of the victims in the files. Different angles, different poses. I don't mention it to my wife. I make colour copies of the photographs for my own personal files. Somebody asks me to make new colour copies of these colour copies for some other files of their own. This keeps me late in the office, alone with a bottle of Lamb's Navy Rum, examining the photographs in the smallest detail. Certain fantasies evolving around the photographs, the different women, the different angles, the different poses. Certain fantasies about these women. Could I have saved them? Could I have got to know them better in wine bars? Could I have left home and taken one of them to the Algarve? Could we have embarked on a unique sexual odyssey together that would have suddenly spiralled hopelessly out of our control?

Well, I don't know . . .

I don't mention it to my wife . . .

She is deaf and dumb. She wouldn't understand.

Blueness

H P Tinker

The blueness of one small blue room.
Overtaken by blueness, eventually. It appears substantial reconstruction and remodelling of your home environment has occurred. Blue leather walls. Blue linoleum floors. Blue metal appliances. Blue glass installations. Obtrusive blueness everywhere. Days and weeks of blueness passing you, sitting there, until somehow you become detached by the blueness, blinded to it. This is an ironic blueness though, you realize: ultra-cool, hip, sardonic, possibly designed by a modern conceptual artist. Sitting alone in this ultra-cool, conceptual blueness . . . eventually asking yourself, *What am I doing here?*

Turning on the wide-screen television with a simple click: Gene Hackman and his huge wide-screen Poseidon Adventure head unnerving you, even though you admired some of his early work. Then Shelley Winters and her fatuous face. Ernest Borgnine and his considerable ballast. Thoroughly unsettled, you shower alone in a bathroom of dark blue stone, thinking about your last ex-lover, the radio blaring, all the insignificant things they did and said drowned out by the radio blaring, drying yourself afterwards on dark blue bath towels, pissing wildly against the porcelain for no good reason.

Growing bored, disconsolate.

Slipping *Black Orpheus* into the DVD player, muting it halfway through when you lose interest. Finding your mind drifting, increasingly weary. In this drifting, weary state compiling a long list of the words and phrases you feel should be banned from common usage. Thinking about sending the list to somebody somewhere, somebody in a position of authority. Erasing the idea from your mind. Instead, studying *Two Children Threatened by a Nightingale* on the wall opposite. Your sense of disquiet expands further. Raw time snagging up around you. Only one way you know how to fill up this time, music: genuine thirties blues, some new-wave country, a collection of abstract jazz rock, a clutch of ambient electro church ballads, several volumes of uninspired guitar music from the early nineties.

Later, reading *Une Semaine de Bonté*, cover to cover, not understanding a word. Later still, drinking Shiraz, a couple of bottles, simultaneously recalling some of your most dearly cherished disappointments in love . . .

Looking out the window, time having passed.

This is the edge of the city, the outskirts of things. Looking outside. Staring deep into the stone-cold heart of a visceral metropolis, an outsider squinting short-sighted into the labyrinthine streets: an emerald city awash with shimmering blue – not actually blue – only awash with shimmering blue because of your expensively installed blue-tinted windows. Small blue people coming and going down there, almost at random. Finding it painful to watch these small blue people disappearing into the urban abyss, swallowed whole, drowning in restaurants, absorbed into the seething media ghetto, never to return. Or so it seems. Whatever; they are lost out there, somewhere in that grim, unrelenting refuge for half-defeated souls. Their trendy carcasses: animal hides caught on the abattoir hooks of lo-fi fashion. Gone. Vanished. Co-opted. Into a city of dark, illuminated rain, professionally faked dawns, broken-down culture, childlike web designers, ironic prostitutes, ersatz line-managers, futile jazz . . . a city of women.

At least that's how it looks from where you're standing. However.

Other people see it differently, you are aware of that. They tell you so. In monochrome bars and overly brightened taxis, during inexorable, inescapable dinner parties. They tell you so in taut, meaningful voices. As if it is important to them. As if you are the crazy one here. *But what do they know?* Unlike them, the soles of your shoes seldom touch these streets any more. The act of putting one foot in front of the other seems repeatedly beyond you. This is not your city. This city is cold and callous and calculating. Reluctantly, more times than you care to remember, you have been forced to drag yourself out there, finding yourself uneasy and uncomfortable on the pavement, melancholy hanging around you: an expansive, unwanted perfume. Dredging the back streets for remnants of forgotten lives and former transactions, renegotiating lost negotiations, digging up corrupt information, exposing corpses in various guises, uncovering hidden people and their alien associates, their misguided agendas . . .

The telephone ringing. A frozen moment. Time seemingly ground to an almost complete halt. Answering the telephone: mouthing *one-two-three-four-five-six-seven-eight-nine-ten* to affect the illusion of being a busy individual caught up with many complex tasks, someone who finds it impossible to get to the phone promptly. Then picking up, taking a deep breath, answering sternly, 'Hello': your voice sounding cold and world-weary without trying, cynical and beat-up – an unusual effect, one you like.

On the other end: a man with a voice; time moving again.

The voice saying things.

Various things. Such as: 'I've heard you can help me . . . I've heard you are the only one who can help me . . . Is it true? . . . Can you help me? . . . Can you be of any assistance at all?'

'Maybe,' you say. 'Maybe I can help you . . .'

(*Note*. The voice is not one you instantly recognize. It's as warm and luxuriant as the inside of a woman. With an edge to it also, another surface: a serrated blade, hangdog tired and driven by a bad case of the blues.)

The voice doesn't pause, carries on:

'Good – you see, I need to acquire your services. Urgently. On behalf of an unnamed second party. I think you might be right for the job. People in certain circles speak well of you, anyway. You come highly recommended. This is what I am trying to assess. Whether you are right for the job. *This* job.'

The voice pleases you. Complimentary words aimed your way down a phone line.

'Go on,' you say, leaning back casually – hard into your chair, the way you have seen paper-thin characters doing on television shows.

'No,' says the voice, sharply. 'I cannot go into that. Not *here*. Not *now*.'

'Oh,' you say, mildly perplexed.

'We must meet. Tonight. That's very important. We must meet *tonight*.'

'OK,' you say, mumbling slightly. 'Where? When?'

The voice then decides these things for you.

You listen to what it has to say, nodding occasionally though you know the voice does not possess the ability to view your actions. Between these involuntary nods, you scribble down some notes, details, scratching them down on a single sheet of blank paper you found lying on the empty table in front of you.

It seems the thing to do.

Then: because your attention span has been shot to pieces, you become distracted. You stop writing words and phrases completely and begin doodling abstract shapes in various corners of the paper. Strange swirls and boxes within boxes, mainly. Shapes that please you, even though they have no rational meaning and you cannot explain why you are drawing them or what their ultimate purpose might be.

Then the voice says 'Goodbye', hangs up.

You are caught out, taken aback, quite aghast, etc., etc.

All memory of what he's said has been wiped clean. You look down at the paper you were scribbling so diligently on. Printed clearly in the middle of the abstract doodling, loops, swirls, boxes, is a time and a place: KARMA BAR 8.30 p.m.

These new words make some new sense to you. But then you study them again. And again. And again. And they start to make no sense at all. They now look abstract. Meaningless. All jumbled up. The more you study them, the more abstract and meaningless they look, like hiero-glyphics.

The street unusually calm and bright, the sky fading and blue, an evening straight out of your childhood. Harsh pavement challenges your shoes – dealing with it, not a problem, because here in the outer arteries of the city you are as good as a king. Standing in your own skin, astronaut feet planted on a solid new surface. You smile: ill-mannered people swarming, not apologizing, not registering your presence.

(*How long is it since you've been out here?* People have better hairstyles now. Less product, more texture. Their clothes have improved in quality too. It seems aesthetics have assumed a greater importance in society.)

These people are heading deeper into the guts of the city and this is what preoccupies them. Their heads are swirling with extraneous thoughts and images. You remain unimportant. They don't see you. In their scheme of things, you are a minor character, irrelevant, relegated to the fringes of whatever half-hearted storyline they are playing out.

Women are everywhere in the street also, you notice.

Passing you. Hundreds of them. In all directions. Some old, some young. Some relapsing, some in irretrievable midlife collapse. Pouring out of cars. Slinking out of shops. All dressed in subtly different combinations of colours and styles. Some wearing trousers, some wearing skirts, some wearing dresses. Some in coats, some without. Some wearing long sleeves, some baring their arms. Some revealing their knees, some practically the whole leg, some with their legs entirely covered. Some with long hair, some with short. Some wearing hats. At first it's a relief to be out there with all these women. With their arms and their legs and their different faces and hairstyles. Then your hands begin shaking with the thought of these women. Their lives. Their hobbies. Their husbands, boyfriends, partners. Their tastes in popular music. Their bank accounts. Their mobile phone numbers. The clothes they have hung in their wardrobes. Their problems. Their teeth.

Telling yourself you're being ludicrous, your hands still shaking all the same.

The Karma Bar, then: its concrete and steel exterior the very height of IRA chic. You know the place, of course, from hastily compiled regional listings magazines. Famously modish, blessed with an eclectic music policy – hardcore pop, sixties lounge-core, fat soul, nineties grunge funk, fluffy hip-hop, eighties jazz, mainstream samba – protected by a grim row of doormen, self-important as a social barrier, all frozen in identical postures, wearing balaclavas, toting Kalashnikovs (a gimmick, you guess). Your entrance, however stylish, is not noted with the slightest flicker or blink. You are the ghost of a former human being, a lost soul, or tax exile: an extra from a George Romero movie.

Inside, everything different. Lush and pink and verdant. Hysterical décor pulsing: a giant vulva, eighties disco thumping off the walls. Not in a pleasing way. Reaching the bar without looking around. Hoping to give the impression you come here frequently. Mirrors. Walls of them. Opposite you: yourself, reflected in a long expanse of mirror – big as a lake. A frozen birthday Polaroid: determined teeth, grim eyes cold as clay. Admiring what you see. (Consciously making the decision to wear these clothes again. Should a suitable moment ever require it.)

Yawning a stray, false yawn unnoticed at the bar.

Socially stranded: not another human being within eyeshot, ordering standard bottled beer, nothing too unexpected. Straining via your peripheral vision meanwhile: seeing some men sitting on high stools, playing computerized card games on small machines fixed along the walls. Lone homosexuals lingering, leaning against rails: *faux* nonchalance. Their unspoken dress code of tight T-shirts wrenched across spilling stomachs, taut over beige trousers. Distracted from your current purpose by a posse of unwanted thoughts entering your head like refugees. Suddenly thinking: 'When I was twenty-one, all I wanted to be was James Bond. But unfortunately for me, I briefly joined a religious cult, discovered Foucault, and it never really happened. Such is life: my life, anyway. And now, when I finish a long day, my *Newsnight*-related fears mix with a loathing of 500-page comic novels about "multi-ethnic" London, written by 47-year-old *Dr Who* fanatics. Sick of trying to pretend, for the sake of it, that I contribute

anything to this world and I am not one of the most point-
less human beings in it. That I'm not some minor irritation
always using the wrong words at the wrong time via the
wrong medium. Does anyone want to know the darker
networks behind these seething simplicities? Does anyone
care what I think? Should I sing of my love of darkened
rooms? Must I produce anything of note within the
framework of my own existence anyway? . . . Personally, I
have absolutely no idea. At the moment, my brain is pure
cat food . . .'

The barman in front of you: deeply smiling, piercing
blue eyes. Consummating with his smiling. A smile carved
out of solid rock, unmoved since the birth of Christ. Opp-
ressive smiling . . . or, homosexual? You cannot say. Recip-
rocating the smile anyway: but only getting midway into it
before feeling the expression drain from your face until
there's nothing left: a blank zone where the smile used to
be . . .

This doesn't perturb the barman too much, however.

He's a professional.

With his barman's face so close up, you are reminded of
many similar barmen you have known: their names and
accents and individual quirks lost to you across the years.
A great sadness weighing down on you, feeling a sense of
loss for these barmen, men from numerous geographical
locations. Then quite suddenly, through this: stranger,
stronger images. Crawling into your mind like the sickness
of somebody else. Deranged mental pictures dangling:
yourself cavorting with the barman, naked arms wrapped
tightly around his white body, loose-fleshed buttocks
heaving. Teeth biting down hard at the nape of your neck . . .

Finding a chair proves easier than you expected . . . waiting there. Freshly discharged urine clawing, piquant, at
your nostrils. Dozens of anorexic girls (and boys) barely
into their twenties in fabulously expensive designer size

eights. Drinking fast. Ordering another. Drinking faster. Ordering again. Hazily the walls of this place protest with pissy aphorisms about love, sex, none resonating with you. Their gaudily ephemeral words are soon indistinct; whatever message they're trying to convey never getting across. Because your pale blue eyes simply refuse to focus any longer and they fade . . .

Another man entirely shows up. Not the man you expect him to be. A man with a moustache. An unconvincing moustache, out of context with the rest of his face. Sharp features. Sharp-cut white suit. Indigo shirt. Indigo tie.

Sitting down, taking a long slug from a glass he is gripping unsteadily.

'I'm glad you could make it,' he says, his voice richly inviting: an old friend from the south coast you feel pleased to meet up with.

'You said it was important,' you say, extending a swift hand.

He shakes it and takes another, longer, harder slug. 'Yes, I did say that – didn't I?'

He continues. 'This is a matter of some importance, as I'm sure you understand. A delicate matter. A matter not to be entered into lightly. It is a matter of an unusual nature. A matter a little out of the ordinary. A matter in which the authorities would be reluctant to get involved. A matter beyond the typical everyday. A matter in which usual procedures will be redundant. A matter in which a more lateral way forward will have to be forged. A matter quite outside of most ordinary matters. I am a go-between. A broker, if you like. I am acting on behalf of a client who is keen to secure the services of somebody like you. Somebody who can act – how can I put it? – outside the usual constraints and considerations of standard practices. This, I can assure you, is not a usual matter. I know what you are thinking: *You need to know exactly what the matter entails.*

You're asking yourself, *What would be involved? What would be required of me?* That is a difficult question to answer. The client I am representing is keen that as little information as possible be exchanged in this preliminary meeting. Of course, in due time, everything will be revealed to you. But at the moment I cannot tell you any more. Quite simply, I'm looking for the right person. That person – I have been informed in certain circles – could be you. You come highly recommended. Now I know what you're thinking: *Who recommended my services?* Well, I couldn't possibly say. There is a certain code of ethics at work here. Let's just say I came to hear of your name in conjunction with another matter. A similar matter. A matter which made your name in certain circles . . .'

'I see,' you say. (Yet. Remembering the antique car dealer who uncannily resembled Andy Warhol; travelling half the world to confront him: Paris. Rome. Berlin. San Francisco. Finding him holed up in a mildly art deco mocked-up thirties luxury cruise liner . . . indulging himself . . . three Japanese girls in a jacuzzi . . . accepting his candid invitation . . . reluctantly joining in . . . but since then things have declined. Things not what they were. Wondering what this secret business is all about. But you are needed here. And perhaps until you are needed by someone, you almost don't physically exist . . .)

'My client is very careful, very private,' the man is saying. 'She wants you to know this matter involves the utmost sensitivity and urgency. It is not a question of time, so much. But there is urgency. The urgency is on her behalf. Do you *comprendez*?'

Face down and retching, head against the table, thinking momentarily you are somebody else, somebody happier. Waking up. Sitting up. A bottle of Captain Morgan's on one side, emptied, heavily defeated. Feeling like morning.

Early morning. The earliest you have woken up for years. The room containing more light than before and the shrill sound of birds singing. From the sound you are unable to deduce exactly what kind of birds they are. Then a thought. How do you know it is morning? How can you reasonably be sure? One thing occurs to you: just how easily you could convince someone it was morning, when actually it wasn't. Artificial light, taped bird songs . . . the previous evening remaining blurred. No recollection of falling asleep. No recollection of sleeping, of dreaming. A long time since you've dreamt: will you ever again? Little snatches of memory knifing at you: a parade of tiny erotic dancers. These memories, real or semi-imagined? For a moment you're not sure. Managing to attach enough of these pin-prick memories together to form a shaky picture of things: your self and your life and the major events of the last few years. Making a cup of coffee, strong as rocket fuel, shaking your foundations. Remembering. Playing a CD: *Collected Silences of the Last Century* from Armistice Day, 1918, to Princess Diana's funeral, 1997. An entire day seeming to pass in silence before putting on another: Bob Dylan, 'Tangled up in Blue'. Looking around the room, looking for something, not recognizing the room, wondering where you are. Eventually your thoughts returning to last night: the phone call, the voice, the meeting, the man, and you decide to prepare yourself in the bathroom. Firstly, you take a shit. An involved procedure. Not at all a simple process. Some degree of difficulty involved, the final push deeply satisfying though, an almost beautiful and euphoric release. Gratified momentarily, you stand up and look down into the light blue toilet bowl, down at the dense brown stool which sits there so perfectly shaped it might have been carved by a commercial artist. Then you pull your trousers up and apply various beauty products to your face, eyes, hair and skin. A process that takes a while.

Finished, studying yourself in the mirror. Looking pretty much as you did before – which makes you wonder why you use these products in the first place. The effect they produce is minimal, visually speaking. But you do smell marginally better than before: a profound, glimmering peppermint aroma.

Your hand. Disembodied. Gripped taut into a fist. Lingering in the air for an unspoken amount of time then crashing forward of its own volition, tapping politely on an imposing door. Waiting. Seconds only before the door is opening onto . . . a woman. Not the kind you expected. A woman who moves her every limb with lightness and grace. (Ballet lessons in her youth?) A young woman. Serious, fanatically well-dressed. In a navy-blue naval suit. Chic. Cut tight to her body. Possibly born into the world in that suit. Standing with the self-assurance of a girl who has always been loaded, never once been rejected. Only twenty, twenty-five at most. Average height. Dark hair, tousled. Beautiful wild eyes, possibly complicated and misunderstood. One snatched look into those eyes simultaneously announcing a twin agenda: love and hate. Standing, staring. Her nose assuming an arrogant tilt. Her lips smeared with toffee-thick red lipstick. Well-situated breasts. Natural, not artfully constructed by a cleverly designed brassière. Standing with the posture of an heiress, beautiful and unmarriable. Pretty legs from ankle to hip. Standing, staring coldly. Perhaps you've seen each other before, in fashionable bars or empty tube stations. She stands in silence, her face skewed with shrewd realism, until she speaks.

'Hello,' she says, using a softly imperious voice, calling whatever shots there are. 'We've been expecting you.'

'Are you –?'

'No,' says the woman.

'Oh –'

'I am her assistant. Come in.'

Shown inside into a long thin hallway. Struck by a vague impression of things rearing up, assaulted by antiques and paintings and silver ornaments in all directions. A stuffed black dog. A portrait of a handsome man with a neatly trimmed beard. An unsolved Rubik's Cube, hopelessly scrambled. Catching sight of a CD case: *The Complete Johnny Mathis*, opened and empty. Everything locked into a seventies timbre, somehow. The general impression being one of comfortable affluence, however.

Gestured down the hallway with a calmly rehearsed smile.

Where she pauses at a tall oak door.

Then opens her lips.

'Actually, she's been expecting you for quite some time,' she says. 'For longer than you can possibly imagine. In fact, she has been *frantically* expecting you. I will discuss things with you, certain points, but I will have to do so later. After you have spoken to her yourself. She wants to see you straight away. She is adamant about that. And it is perhaps best that you speak to her first. Perhaps it is best this way. That I say nothing. But please do not be disconcerted by what you find in there. Or by what she says . . .'

She smiles and pushes the door open with the officiousness of a legal secretary, enabling you to steal your first glimpse of what lies beyond. Not seeing much. Sensing something instead. Something else. A haze of gentle light drifting in from the other side, a thin trace of perfume not there before . . .

'You can go through now,' she says, revealing two rows of perfect white teeth.

About the Editor

NICHOLAS ROYLE is the author of five novels and more than a hundred short stories. His 'chilling and exhilarating' Belgian noir thriller *Antwerp* was published by Serpent's Tail in June 2004. He has edited twelve anthologies including *The Time Out Book of New York Short Stories*, *The Ex Files: New Stories About Old Flames* and the bestselling *A Book of Two Halves*.